Guarded Prognosis

AUTHOR'S NOTES:

When I got the editorial letter for my first novel, I couldn't believe it needed improvement. The publisher had bought the book, so why did I need to rewrite it? I've found since that time, in the decade and more that I've been writing professionally, that a novel can always be improved. This one is no exception, and I thank my first reader, Kay Mabry for suggesting to me how to do it. The novel has been rewritten, following her recommendations, and is the better for it.

As is the case with all my indie-published work, my thanks go to Dineen Miller for designing and executing a great cover, Barbara Scott for applying her editorial genius, and Virginia Smith for getting this book into print.

I appreciate all the writers who, over the years, have unselfishly mentored and supported me along this road to writing. There are too many to name, but you know who you are.

Over a decade ago, when I set out to write a book about my struggles after the death of my first wife, a book that was published as *The Tender Scar*, I had no idea that God would lead me along this path of writing. I've been fortunate enough now to see the publication of twelve novels and four novellas, in addition to the non-fiction book I originally set out to craft. I'm amazed and a bit awe-struck by all this. But, as always, *Soli Deo Gloria*—to God be the glory.

Guarded Prognosis

RICHARD L. MABRY, MD

GUARDED PROGNOSIS

The men sitting in adjacent chairs looked out of place in the corner of the surgeon's waiting room. It wasn't just that they didn't have visible bandages, or that neither of them winced or evidenced pain. While many of the men and women waiting to see Dr. Caden Taggart bore expressions that said they either needed the surgeon's attention or had already experienced it, these two men presented themselves the way drug salesmen do—sitting patiently, idly thumbing through magazines, almost bored.

When he came to the front desk to hand off the chart of the patient he'd just seen, Caden glanced at the men in the corner. He noted they wore dark suits and white shirts. Their conservative ties were snugged against their cleanly shaven necks, and their lace-up shoes had probably been shined this morning. He didn't know who they were—perhaps police, maybe FBI—but their presence in his office worried him. He didn't think he had anything to fear, but then again...

Caden leaned closer to his receptionist. "Donna, who are those two men?"

"I didn't get their names. They flashed ID and badges but stowed them before I got a good look. They said they had to see you. When I asked them why, they said they'd discuss it with you."

"They didn't give you any clue?"

She lowered her voice even further, although no one seemed to be paying attention to the conversation. "They wouldn't say anything beyond what I've told you. They took a seat, and that's where they've been since then."

"When's my next patient?"

"In ten minutes. She's post-op appendectomy and arrived a bit early. Ruth just took her back to do vital signs."

"Why don't I see them while I'm waiting? Give me a moment, then send them back."

As he entered his office, Caden glanced at the cherrywood desk his father had given him when he opened his surgical practice two years ago. He wondered if Dr. Henry Taggart ever considered that there were more important gifts he could share with his son than those bought with money.

Caden's thoughts were interrupted by the arrival of the two strangers. "Gentlemen." He inclined his head toward the two chairs across the desk from him. He decided not to say anything more for fear he might indicate the nervousness he felt. Let them talk.

As he sat down behind the desk, Cade took the measure of his visitors. The man on his left was probably in his late 50s. His dark hair was cut short and showed a hint of gray at the temples. The other man, about a decade younger than the first, was blond. Other than that, they were very much alike—average build, no facial hair, clothes neat but not flashy.

The older man pulled out a small leather wallet and held it out to Caden, who noted the badge and ID card it contained. "I'm agent Darren Neilson, Drug Enforcement Agency." He nodded toward the man on his left. "This is agent Jerry Harwell."

Harwell offered his badge and credentials but said nothing.

Caden looked at the ID cards. They carried the names the two men had given, the pictures matched the facial features he saw across the desk, and the badges said Drug Enforcement Agency. Of course, he'd never seen real badges or credentials from the agency. He had no idea of the authenticity of their credentials. He decided that, for now, he'd accept the identities the men across the desk presented.

Caden took a deep breath and waited for them to explain their presence. The practice of medicine had so many regulations now, he wondered which one of them he'd inadvertently broken. He was certain he'd filled out all the forms, paid all the required fees, instituted the necessary safeguards. As a general surgeon, he sometimes prescribed narcotics, but not a lot, and always with no refills. What could the DEA want with him?

Neilson pulled a piece of paper from an inner coat pocket. Evidently, he was going to be the spokesman for the two. "Do you remember a patient named John Pace?" He didn't wait for Caden to respond before he went on. "Emilia Smith? Bart Wilkerson? Ed Cowgill?"

"I see lots of people. Sometimes I operate on them. Then, with few exceptions, they go back to their referring doctor. I don't really have any long-term relationships with my patients. But, no, none of those names strikes a chord with me."

The older agent laid the list on the desk and pulled out another one, which he only glanced at. "The maximum prescription for Vicodin and similar narcotics is eight a day for a month, or 240 tabs. Pace and Smith got a script from you recently for that amount."

Caden guessed he'd heard those numbers before, but they weren't applicable to his practice, so he'd ignored them. "I don't—"

Neilson talked right over him. "For patients with breakthrough pain, you can give an additional 120 tabs. That's what Wilkerson and Cowgill got, also in a prescription signed by you."

Caden was shaking his head before the agent finished. "This has to be a mistake. I don't think I've ever written such a script."

Just then there was a tap on the door and Caden's nurse stuck her head in. "Doctor, your patient is ready in treatment room one."

"Please tell the patient I'll be another few minutes, Rose." He waited until she withdrew and the door was closed before he addressed the two men across the desk from him. "Was my signature on those prescriptions? Was my DEA number used?"

Rather than answer Caden's question, Agent Harwell drew an official-looking document from inside his coat, unfolded it, and held it out for the doctor to read. "This is a death certificate for a patient. Look at the cause of death."

Caden leaned forward. The line in question read, "Cardiac and respiratory arrest due to drug administration." He read it twice before looking at Harwell. "This is unfortunate, but what does it have to do with me?"

Harwell returned the death certificate to his pocket. "Fentanyl, usually as a patch, is sometimes given for severe pain. But the latest thing for drug addicts is graduating to a mixture of heroin and fentanyl. This man, and more like him, died after using such a combination. And the fentanyl was obtained using your name and DEA number."

"Whoa! I'm certain that I've never written a prescription for fentanyl in any form."

"Are you sure? Did you ever give someone else authorization to use your name and number? Under any circumstance?"

The doctor recalled hearing that an innocent man has nothing to fear from the law. That might be true in theory, but right now he felt anything but secure. "Do I need a lawyer?"

Neilson took up the conversation now. His tone was that of a favorite uncle, trying to reassure a worrying nephew. "You can call your attorney if you think you need to. But if you're innocent …"

Who would I call? I don't know a lawyer. Certainly not one I trust in a situation like this.

Before Caden could speak, the agent went on. "If you cooperate we can keep this simple. On the other hand, if you want to complicate things …"

The doctor felt his pulse climbing while his throat seemed to close up. *No, I don't want to complicate things. If I don't call a lawyer, if I cooperate, maybe they'll go away, and this will all be over.*

"I guess we'll keep this simple. What do you need from me?"

Caden was a full hour behind schedule when he got around to seeing patients again. Although he was pretty good at compartmentalizing problems and devoting his undivided attention to the situation at hand, in the back of his mind he kept going over his conversation with the two men.

They'd be back for more in a few days. Apparently, they planned to check records, procedures, everything about the practice. They gave no indication that Caden was involved in the illegal prescribing, but the men stopped short of assuring him he was innocent. Should he consult an attorney? Again, he didn't know one to call. And what would he tell them if he did? No, he decided to go with Neilson's suggestion. Keep things simple. After all, he was innocent.

Noontime came and went, but eventually the waiting room was empty. "Do I have a break here?" he asked his nurse, Rose.

She looked at her watch. "About three quarters of an hour before your next patient. I'm going to run up to the corner deli. Want me to bring you a sandwich?"

"No, I'm not particularly hungry," Caden said.

"Oh, Dr. Taggart." Donna approached from the front desk, a pink call slip in her hand. "This message came in about an hour ago. I was going to interrupt you, but the caller said to give it to you at your next break. It wasn't urgent. And you'd know the number."

He took the piece of paper she handed him. It said, "Call Dr. Henry Taggart at his office." So far as Caden was concerned, when his father took time from his own surgical practice to call, the urgency was implied. Although he called Caden at home occasionally, he couldn't remember a call from his father to his office since he'd opened his practice.

"I'll phone him now," Caden said, and turned away.

He dropped into the swivel chair behind his desk, pulling the phone toward him and trying to suppress his apprehension. His father had said that his son knew his dad's office number. Actually, that wasn't true. He tried to remember when he'd last called that number, but he couldn't. Caden found the number in his middle desk drawer on one of his father's cards. With a silent prayer, he punched in the numbers.

"Dr. Taggart's office."

"Hi Jean," he said. "This is Caden Taggart. My dad called me. Is he with a patient?"

"He's just finishing. Can you hold for a minute? I know he wants to talk with you."

There was nothing particularly unusual in Jean's words, but nevertheless something sounded...different. He couldn't put his finger on it, but it definitely set off his radar.

It wasn't long before Dr. Henry Taggart picked up the phone. "Caden. Thanks for calling back."

Caden started with the question that jumped to the mind of most children when they receive a phone call from an older parent. "Dad, is everything okay? Has something happened to you or mom?"

"So far as I know, your mother is fine. I visited the nursing home this past weekend. The staff is taking good care of her, and her doctor checks on her periodically." He paused. "I'm afraid I'm the one who has a little problem."

The sinking feeling Caden experienced was like the one he got in a glass elevator that went down too rapidly. For Henry Taggart to admit he had a problem—even a "little one"—wasn't good.

"I've been having some vague digestive symptoms," the elder Taggart said. "It went on long enough that I finally checked with my internist. He poked and prodded, then persuaded me to have a GI series. After I—"

"Dad, tell me what Dr. Geist found."

"He thinks it's most likely pancreatic carcinoma."

Caden felt acid rise in the back of his throat. His pulse sounded like a windstorm in his ears. Pancreatic carcinoma. To a doctor, this translated into a virtual death sentence. The diagnosis was almost never made in time to do anything more than give palliative or experimental treatment. The son in Caden wanted to drop everything and rush to his father's side. The physician, on the other hand, began to think through the various treatment options and the medical personnel and places that administered them.

"Fred wants me to see the oncologists at the university medical center here in Dallas," Henry said. "They've got a good team of specialists over there, and I'm sure they're ready to jump in—if I let them."

"What do you mean 'if'? Aren't you planning to let the doctors handle this?"

"Possibly," Henry said. "But we both know that if this is pancreatic cancer, the outlook is pretty grim."

"But it's not—"

Before Caden could finish his sentence, his father added, "And I may need your help."

"I'll do anything I can to help, but there are good people at the medical center there. Do you want me to come to Dallas? Would you like me—"

"No, I don't want you to treat me. I want you to help me if I decide to commit suicide."

2

The smell coming from the oven brought a smile to Beth's face. She was glad she'd learned to cook... although not from her mother's teaching. No, the best thing her mother made for dinner was reservations. After she was married, Beth had read books, watched TV programs, and exchanged tips with other wives as Caden completed his residency. Her cooking may have started out as suspect, but by now she was sure her husband had no complaints about the food she set before him.

Beth felt something brush against her ankles. She looked down at the tan kitten and smiled. "Sorry, Kitty. No time to play. Caden will be home soon." She heard the door open and close. "There he is now."

When her husband came through the door into the kitchen, Beth dried her hands on the apron she wore. She turned to look at him, and when she saw his expression her heart fell. "I'm guessing something really bad happened today."

She turned back toward the stove, but Caden caught her from behind in a hug that lasted longer than usual. He kissed the nape of her neck. "You don't know the half of it."

"Well, I will when you tell me about it." She put down the spoon she had picked up and gave her husband a proper kiss. "Supper needs about twenty more minutes in the oven. Let's go into the living room so you can unload."

Beth was used to Caden's tales of the day's adventures. Actually, she enjoyed the second-hand exposure to the medical world. She wished she was back working as a nurse, but that wasn't what Caden wanted. When they moved to Freeman, he'd told her he wanted her to be a stay-at-home wife ... and mother.

As they headed for the sofa, the place they usually sat and shared stories of the day, Beth could tell Caden seemed lost in thought. She eased down in her usual place, patted the cushion beside her, and said, "Tell me about it."

"I talked with Dad today."

Beth's eyebrows shot up. "Did he come by?"

"No, he called."

Since Henry Taggart's calls to his son were about as frequent as a lunar eclipse, Beth knew something unusual was going on. She didn't realize how unusual until Caden finished his recital of what his father had told him.

"Carcinoma of the pancreas?" She tried to keep from showing the fear every medical professional felt when they heard those words. "But it's still presumptive, based on an exam and one set of X-rays. He hasn't had confirmation of the diagnosis yet. Right?"

"Right, but both his internist and he seemed pretty sure."

"Until it's more than a suspected diagnosis, there's still hope," Beth said. "And even if it does turn out to be pancreatic carcinoma, we don't know what Henry's clinical course will be."

True, the diagnosis mentioned was oftentimes a death sentence, but Beth, as a trained nurse, also knew that it was utter foolishness to say that a person had such-and-such a number of weeks or months to live. Predictions like that were never made in medicine, despite the way the movies and novels showed doctors issuing such exact pronouncements.

"His internist wants him to see some specialists at the medical center there in Dallas," Caden said. "We should know more about it soon. He mainly called to tell me about the diagnosis."

"How's he taking it?"

"Hard to tell, but what he asked me sort of gave me a clue." Caden paused, as though getting up his courage for the next sentence. "He asked me about helping him commit suicide."

Beth felt like someone had sucker-punched her in the gut. If the diagnosis was correct, she realized that the outcome didn't look good, but it was far from set in stone. Finally, she spoke. "What did you tell him?"

"I sort of let it hang there. I … I had something else on my mind, but I promised him we'd talk again soon."

The buzzer on the oven went off. Beth got up but put her hand on Caden's shoulder to keep him sitting. "Let me turn the heat down to warm. I think you'd better tell me what else happened today to divert your attention. Be right back."

Caden half-rose when Beth hurried back into the room, wiping her hands on a kitchen towel.

She resumed her seat on the sofa. "Now tell me what else happened today."

He took a deep breath. He didn't want her worrying about the office, but this was too big not to share. "Two men came by to see me—agents from the Drug Enforcement Agency…"

He told it all. Beth didn't say anything, but Caden could almost see the wheels turning as he spoke. Beth had never encountered any problem for which she didn't have a solution, and when he finished speaking, he was certain she'd tell him how she'd handle this. He was used to this, but he didn't mind, because she was right most of the time.

Beth waited until he was through before she spoke. "It sounds like they're not so much after you as interested in your office routine. It appears you're probably not the one under the gun."

"I hope you're right, although if I'm not the one they're interested in, someone in that office has been doing this stuff. I just can't believe it."

"Think you should consult an attorney?" Beth asked.

"I thought about it, but I don't know one—certainly not well enough to trust him with something like this. It's … It's kind of embarrassing. Then one of the agents suggested I keep it simple and let them look around. So that's what I decided to do." Caden ran his fingers through his hair. "I haven't figured out how I'll let the agents ask questions without the nurses and other doctors knowing the DEA is snooping around."

"I think maybe what I'd do is say they're doctors who wanted to look at your office's operation. That should cover it."

Caden nodded. "I suppose I can do that. I can introduce Neilson as a doctor who's been in academia in another state. He's thinking of setting up private practice here, and he wants to see how ours functions. Harwell might move here and go in with him, but he'd like to see how things are done in Freeman."

"Now back to the other problem," Beth said. "When are we going to drive to Dallas to see your father?"

Caden had been turning that over, but his plans had never gotten very far. "With this DEA thing, I don't know about leaving."

"We have every reason to go, and this weekend is a good time. By the way, and this really isn't off-topic, I talked with my mother today."

"Anything important, or just the usual complaining?"

"Caden, I realize you and Mother don't see eye to eye, but she's really got a good heart."

He realized that was probably true. Maybe he should be kinder in his remarks about her mother. But right now, he didn't feel like dealing with one of his wife's sermons. "What did you all talk about? Did her conversation cover all the points in the Beverly Cummings trifecta—you're wasting your nurses' training, why haven't we given her a grandchild, and when are we coming to see them?"

"As a matter of fact, she mentioned all three. I didn't respond to the first two, but I told her we'd try to get to south Texas to see them soon—this weekend if possible."

"But—"

Beth raised a finger to stop her husband. "Hear me out. Tomorrow is Friday. Is the DEA going to start then?"

"No. They decided next Monday would be soon enough. They'll start looking then."

"You're not on call this weekend. I think we should go to Dallas on Saturday to see your father. It's just an hour's drive, and I'm embarrassed you haven't seen him in so long. We need to go there, offer support, do what families do."

Caden thought back on the times he'd have appreciated a visit—or even a call—from his father. But he realized that just because Henry Taggart hadn't done what he should was no reason for his son to repeat the behavior. "I suppose you're right."

"Is there any reason you can't be gone this weekend?"

Caden thought about it. His colleague, Dr. Ann Russell, was on call this weekend, but there was nothing special to tell her. "I think it will be fine. Do you want me to call Dad to tell him to expect us?"

"That would be nice. And I'll phone Mother and explain why we won't be coming to see them this weekend. I'll tell her your dad has some problems but won't get specific. Not yet." Beth stood. "Now, let's have some of that casserole I cooked before it's too dry to enjoy."

Caden didn't feel very hungry, but the food Beth prepared did smell good. And he had to admit that he felt better now that he'd shared his problems with her. Wasn't there something in the Bible about sharing bad things? He'd have to ask Beth about it. That was her thing, not his.

Beth watched her husband load the suitcases into his SUV on Saturday morning. She wasn't concerned about whether the DEA agents would find any irregularities involving her husband. That was one of the things she found endearing about him—he was definitely what used to be called a "straight arrow." No, her mind was on this trip to Dallas.

She waited until they had left the city limits of Freeman before she started the conversation. "It will be good to see Henry. He needs his family around him at a time like this." Beth took a deep breath. "And I think we should see your mother while we're there as well."

Her husband's face flinched when she mentioned visiting his mother. "I'm going. Will you go with me?"

Ever since Nancy's stroke about two years ago, when the neurologist told Henry his wife would never be a sentient human again, she had lived in Sunset Rest to receive the constant nursing care she needed. Beth had visited her every month. And each time, when Beth asked him if he'd like to accompany her, Caden had said, "I don't want to see my mother looking like that. Can't you go by yourself?"

Of course, she'd also suggested they take a weekend to visit Caden's father as well. But her husband always found some excuse for not going. Well, this time they were both traveling to Dallas, and she was determined Caden would see both his father *and* his mother.

If he went with her to Sunset Rest to see his mom, Beth knew this would be one small victory in her battle. She considered taking the conversation further, trying to convince Caden that God would see him through these crises—his father's diagnosis, his mother's status, the DEA agents looking around his office. But she decided not to go there right now. She was aware that her husband wasn't on speaking terms with God. She wasn't sure how to get Caden to take the first step toward repairing that breach. But she'd continue to work on it.

"I'm in. We're going back on Monday to look around the office."

"How did he take it?"

"Surprised and a little scared, just as you predicted. We'll be there for several days, and I'm going to make certain there's nothing that points to the racket we have going on."

"How are you going to wind this up? What's your end game?"

"I'd like to go through the investigation and say that any fake prescribing of narcotics has stopped. That would let the higher-ups direct their attention to another area. After all, their assets are stretched pretty thin. We're just unlucky they chose this one to look into."

"But if you can't give the practice a clean bill of health—"

"The alternative plan is to have Dr. Taggart tragically die, preferably by his own hand, leaving behind a note taking responsibility for the prescriptions coming from his office."

"I'd hate for it to come to that."

"Because it would mean his death?"

"No. Because it's so much simpler the other way."

"We'll call the second scenario Plan B. I'm prepared to put either one in motion. It just depends on how this plays out."

As Caden pulled into the driveway of his childhood home in the University Park section of Dallas, memories came flooding back. The neighborhood was upscale, and the house was as nice as those of the neighbors, but Caden never thought of it in those terms. To him the house and its location weren't important. What made it home to Caden was the presence of his mother, the woman who always seemed to be around when he needed her.

He guessed what he remembered most was how his mom never missed one of his activities, especially the baseball games. Sure, his father had tried—even made it to one or two of the games—but a lot of the time he'd been too busy with his practice.

Henry Taggart always had an apology ready for his son after he failed to show up, and Caden had tried to shrug off these absences. He knew that most fathers couldn't get away from work to be at the high school games, which most often were held right after school. But deep in his heart, Caden always wished his father could be there. He would have given anything for his dad's praise, but the opportunity never came.

There'd been the time his high school coach told him he'd be the starting pitcher in the district playoff game. That was an important contest, one that would decide the championship. Caden hurried home to give both parents the news, and Henry Taggart assured his son he wouldn't miss the game. But he did.

"Sorry, Caden. An emergency came up," he explained. "I'm sure you understand."

Caden had pushed back the tears forming in his eyes. "That's okay, Dad." Then he couldn't help adding, "Mom was there." She had always been there.

Thinking about his childhood made Caden renew his resolve not to be like his father. He'd pay attention to his family. There was only Beth right now, but there'd be children as soon as he got his practice established.

Beth put her hand on Caden's arm, bringing him back to the present. "Ready for this?"

"I'm as ready as I'll ever be," he said.

As they approached the front door, Caden's memory flashed back to the first time he came home from college. His mother had met him at the door with open arms. How he wished she could be there again. He stepped onto the porch, but before he could touch the knob a woman opened the door of the house in which Caden had lived for so many years. But it wasn't his mother.

3

The Nancy Taggart that Caden remembered was a petite lady, with hair the shade of red-brown most people called auburn. She smiled often, not only with her face, but with her sparkling green eyes. The woman who opened the door for Caden was about the same age as his mother, but the resemblance stopped there. She was a bit taller than Mom. Her hair was dark blonde and cut short. Rimless glasses partially hid gray eyes. And her voice was a soft contralto, not the lilting soprano he remembered as his mother's.

The woman who opened the door was no stranger to Caden, but in his mind she only represented a name that occasionally came up, a voice on the phone, a presence in his dad's office. She shouldn't be the person who welcomed him to this house.

"Caden," she said as she stepped forward to give him a hug. "It's good to see you." She turned to Beth, who waited a step behind her husband. "And Beth. I'm glad you both could come."

It took Caden a moment to react. "Sorry, Jean. You took me by surprise." He turned to Beth. "You remember Jean Kirkpatrick—Dad's nurse." He bore down on the last word, as though by doing so he could emphasize how out of place she seemed here in his father's home.

"Of course. You were at our wedding." The two women exchanged hugs.

"Is that Caden?" Henry Taggart called from deeper in the house.

Jean followed Caden and Beth into the study where his dad sat by the window in the armchair that had always been off limits to the younger Taggart. "Don't sit there. That's your father's chair," his mother had said repeatedly.

His father stood—were his movements a bit slower than usual?—and moved toward his son and daughter-in-law.

"I was surprised to get your call last night," Henry said. "There was no need for you to come. But I'm glad you did."

The doctor and the son within Caden fought, and the son won. He didn't look for a yellow cast in the whites of his dad's eyes. Caden didn't scan for early signs of weight loss in the man's arms or an increase in his abdominal girth. No, he was just glad to see his dad. He wondered how many more times he'd be able to see him, talk with him.

His father's dark hair was wavy like his son's, but his hairline had receded a bit and there was some gray at the temples, something that Caden didn't recall from his last visit. Had his father shrunk since their last meeting, or was it only Caden's imagination at work? Was the change due to aging or to cancer?

Caden stepped forward and hugged his father. "Dad, we're here for you."

His father nodded at Caden's words, then moved to embrace Beth. "It's so good to see you both." He waved them to chairs.

"Let me get lunch on the table," Jean said from her position on the periphery of the group. She turned to the visitors. "You haven't eaten yet, have you?"

"No, we came straight here." Beth didn't bother sitting down. Instead, she turned toward Jean. "Let me help you with lunch." Both women left the room without a glance behind them.

Caden sat down and leaned forward, his elbows on his knees. "Dad, you're looking good. I'm glad to see that. Now that we're here, tell me what you know about your diagnosis."

"Get right down to it, do you? That's the surgeon in you, I guess," his dad said. "Next week I'll see one of the specialists at the medical center here in Dallas. Dr. Geist and I think they'll do a CAT scan first to confirm what the GI series showed."

"But—"

"Yes." His father nodded. "You and I both know a biopsy and tissue exam is the gold standard. That will answer the question once and for all of whether I have pancreatic ca."

"But not an open biopsy—no surgery. Right?"

"Right." The smile that accompanied his dad's response was minimal—more of a grimace. "The oncologist will probably do an endoscopic ultrasound and needle biopsy." He placed his hand before his mouth and mimed swallowing. "I just swallow a long tube, they use an ultrasound probe at the end of it to look around, get a few needle biopsy specimens, and it's over. No general anesthetic. No surgical procedure."

"I suppose you'll be sedated for the procedure, which means you'll need someone to drive you home," Caden said. He pulled out his smart phone. "Tell me when it's scheduled. Beth or I can come back here then."

"No need. Jean will drive me to and from the testing, and I can call you after we get the results."

Part of Caden realized it might not be practical for him to cancel his schedule and help his father. But the other part was a little upset, not just that someone else was doing what he wished he was able to do, but because Jean was playing a more important role in his father's life than just being his office nurse. It was bad enough that his mother was in a coma. A thought that had festered in Caden's mind since they'd arrived now began to bloom. Was his dad planning for Jean to take Nancy Taggart's place in other ways?

Beth saw that Jean didn't really need any assistance as she moved confidently around the kitchen putting the finishing touches on lunch.

"I suppose you'll eat at the kitchen table," Jean said. "Henry hates to use the dining room. Says it's too formal."

"Fine." Beth took the folded napkins Jean had set down on the far end of the table and began to lay places.

"I imagine this was a shock," Jean said over her shoulder as she ladled soup into bowls. She pointed to a drawer. "You'll find silverware in there."

It took Beth a moment to realize Jean was talking about learning Henry's probable diagnosis, not his relationship with his nurse. "It was. We're all anxious to see what the work-up shows."

"Henry might fuss and say there's no need for Caden and you to come here, but I know he's glad you did." Jean inclined her head toward the now-filled soup bowls. "Want to put those on the table? I have some cornbread coming out of the oven in a minute."

Jean had set out three napkins and dished up three bowls of soup. "Aren't you eating with us?" Beth asked her.

"No. I'm happy to fix you all some lunch, but this is family time. I'll leave you to talk."

Jean put a trivet in the center of the table and set a pan of cornbread on it. "The butter is in the refrigerator. I'll pour the drinks. Henry will want iced tea. How about you and Caden?"

Beth set the butter on the table next to the cornbread. "Tea will be fine."

"I'll tell the men lunch is ready, then I'll be on my way," Jean said. "It was good to see you again, although not under these circumstances."

As she waited in the kitchen, Beth wondered if there were other surprises ahead for Caden … and for her.

Caden looked around when he sensed someone entering the room.

"Beth is putting lunch on the table," Jean said. "I'll be going now. Leave the dishes when you've finished. I'll come back later to clean up."

Caden noted that she didn't hug or kiss Henry, but the look they shared told him there was something there. Before Jean could leave the room, Caden said, "Dad, while we're here, I think Beth and I will go see Mother at the nursing home. Want to come?"

"I go every week, Son. But I'm glad you'll be going."

As soon as Jean left the room, Caden moved into a part of the discussion he'd thus far avoided. He hadn't yet touched on the question of Henry ending his own life—and Caden's role in it. Was his father serious when he talked about suicide if it came to that? For a fleeting moment, Caden thought maybe if he didn't mention it, the subject would fade away. *Yeah, right.*

Caden looked around to make certain no one else was in the room before he spoke again. "Dad, I want you to do two things for me. First, I promise not to interfere with the doctors who will be treating you, but I want your assurance that you'll keep me posted on what they say before you make any final decision about treatment."

His father rose from his chair and stood for a moment in silence. His countenance revealed nothing. "All right. So long as you realize that I'm the one who'll make that decision, not you."

"And the other thing that's important to me is that you put the idea of suicide out of your head for now. There'll be enough time to consider it further down the line if it comes to that." *But I hope it won't.*

"We'll talk about it when I think it's time to talk about it. You've never told me no in your life, and I imagine you won't start if I ask for one last favor."

When they reached the table, his father went to the chair at the head—the same one he'd occupied during all the years Caden was growing up. "Let's sit down and eat before the food that Jean prepared gets cold."

Beth looked at Caden, who inclined his head toward the chair to his father's left. She sat down, and he took the place across the table from her. There was an empty chair at the other end of the table—the one his mother had typically occupied. Caden looked at it and almost cried.

"Caden, would you ask the blessing?" his father said.

Caden couldn't recall the last time he'd prayed audibly, and he certainly didn't feel like praying now. As if the specter of a government investigation looming in the background wasn't enough, he'd discovered that his father had received a tentative diagnosis of a fatal disorder. And not only did his mother lie unresponsive in a nursing home, but it appeared that a woman he'd thought of only in her role as his father's nurse was now slipping into a different role. Nothing was the same anymore. Everything was bad and getting worse. What was there to thank God for?

Then Caden looked across the table at Beth, who was smiling at him as though she were saying, "You can do it." He felt like gritting his teeth, but instead Caden bowed his head and asked God to bless the food. Then he prayed that God would meet the needs of each person sitting there. He thought about praying specifically for strength and wisdom for himself. But he didn't, although he felt sure that was exactly what Beth was silently asking God for on his behalf right now.

"I'm glad you're going with me to see your mother," Beth said as she buckled her seat belt.

Caden started the car, shrugged, but made no response.

Beth thought back to the times she had visited Nancy Taggart at Sunset Rest. Those visits had consisted mainly of sitting at the bedside, holding the woman's inert hand, and trying to think of something to say. She always came away from those times wishing Caden had come with her. But his refusal was based on his contention that he wanted to remember his mother as she'd been.

Her mind went back to the last time she'd seen Caden's mother—she started to say, "alive," but that wasn't accurate. She supposed the last time she had seen the real Nancy Taggart was at Beth's wedding with Caden. The person she pictured in her mind was that woman—the one with the vivacious smile, the one who'd looked up proudly at her son as he and Beth hurried down the aisle together after exchanging vows.

Nancy Taggart was a woman Beth would have traded her own mother for in a heartbeat. Whereas Beverly Cummings never missed an opportunity to get in a veiled criticism of the man her daughter married, Nancy was kind and caring, a lovely person inside and out. Then the sudden rupture of a small blood vessel in her head had turned her into…the best words Beth could come up with were that her mother-in-law was now in a vegetative state. Although the woman's body was alive and might be for many years to come, she was in a deep coma, totally unresponsive to all but the most painful stimuli.

Why couldn't the intracranial hemorrhage have killed her? Beth had wondered this so often that she no longer was shocked by the thought, although she never expressed it. The neurosurgeon had been able to control the bleeding and relieve the pressure on the brain, but not before irreversible damage occurred. The medical team had been successful in stabilizing Caden's mother, but days turned into weeks with no improvement. The family prayed for a miracle that didn't happen. Nancy had gone from the recovery room to the ICU to a regular room, but there'd been no change.

Now at age 57, Nancy Taggart lay unresponsive in this nursing home. She was able to breathe without the support of a respirator. Her circulation was good. The staff took every precaution to protect her skin from breaking down. She was fed regularly, a special liquid administered through a tube surgically placed into her stomach via a small abdominal incision. Nancy might live another twenty years or more … and during that time her husband and son would also live with the situation, undoubtedly wondering, as did Beth, "What if?"

Caden pulled the car into a space in front of the nursing home and parked.

She looked at her husband. "Ready?"

Caden nodded, unfastened his seat belt, and exited the car.

Hadn't Henry told them he came every week? Beth wondered how he'd been able to tolerate sitting at the bedside of the woman he loved, seeing her this way, trying to think of things to say.

Nancy was in a private room, one that was bright, airy, and clean. Beth was pleased with that, contrasting it with the nursing home where her aunt spent the last two years of her life. There were no people in wheelchairs lining the halls. The doors to many of the rooms were open, with the sound of music or images from the TV leaking into the hallway. But the rooms themselves were otherwise quiet.

Nancy Taggart lay motionless in the center of the bed. Her eyes were half-closed, directed toward the ceiling, blinking occasionally. Beth wondered if any of the images those eyes saw registered on the woman's brain.

Caden walked to the edge of the bed where his mother lay. He took her hand and said, "Mom, it's me—Caden. I brought Beth with me. You remember Beth." His voice caught, and he seemed to take a moment to recover his composure. "Anyway, we were in town to visit Dad, and I couldn't let the opportunity go by without seeing you too."

Nancy didn't look toward him when Caden spoke. So far as Beth could tell, the woman didn't respond to her son's touch by so much as a twitch of her hand. It was as though she were in suspended animation, with no more movement or change of facial expression than a department store mannequin.

Often patients in Nancy's condition displayed claw-like hands and drawn extremities that resulted from long-term disuse. There was only minimal evidence of them here, probably due to regular passive motion activities by a physical therapist. Beth was certain that Henry Taggart spared no expense on his wife, even though she was undoubtedly unaware of any of it.

Nancy's hair had been shaved for the surgery that followed her intracranial bleeding episode, and when it grew back most of the naturally auburn color had changed to brown interspersed with gray. Today her hair was combed and styled. She wore a flattering shade of lipstick. Her gown was a pleasant shade of coral, not the generic white ones Beth was used to seeing on hospital patients.

If one looked past the makeup and the lovely gown, it was possible to see the tube from a catheter, snaking under the covers, leading to a urine bag hanging unobtrusively at the end of the bed.

And despite everything else, Beth noted a faint odor in the air, one that aerosols and electronic air fresheners couldn't eliminate. Although the smell was barely discernible, there was no doubt about its composition—a mixture of urine, feces, and decay. There was no mistaking the fact that Sunset Rest was a place where patients came to die.

"Beth and I had lunch with Dad," Caden said to his mother. "He's doing fine. He told me he comes by here regularly." In the brief silence that followed, he seemed to be searching for something more to say. "You're looking good. I guess they're taking good care of you."

Beth tried to join in, but if Caden was having a hard time thinking of subjects for conversation, her own struggle left her feeling like she'd been butting her head against a wall. She could hardly keep from crying. Beth began to realize why Caden had avoided visiting his mother in the nursing home. He said he wanted to remember Nancy as she'd been, and Beth could see why. This was merely the residuals of the woman he'd known growing up.

Beth's visits on a monthly basis had been difficult, and she was only related to Nancy by marriage. How could Caden do it—spend time talking with this woman who had been an integral part of his life, was once vibrant and alive, but now was merely an inanimate shell? What must it have been like for Henry, coming here week after week?

Once more the thought Beth couldn't get out of her mind came to the surface. How much nicer it would be for everyone if Nancy Taggart were dead.

Finally, Beth could stand it no longer. She turned away from the bed and lowered the volume of her voice until it was almost inaudible. "How much longer do you think we should stay?" she asked her husband. "Is your mother even aware of us?"

Caden shook his head. In an equally soft voice, he said, "No one knows. Science doesn't have the answer to whether a person in a coma can hear or perceive outside stimuli, but just in case, I want to talk to her." He looked down. "Actually, I guess this is as much for me as for her."

"Then we'll stay as long as you want to," Beth said.

4

At the Taggart house, Caden turned the knob of the front door but found it locked. When no one answered the bell, he fished in his pocket and brought out a single key, which he used to let them in. "I'm glad I remembered to bring this."

"You've kept it all these years?"

"Yeah. Even after you and I were married, I guess I thought of this as my home." *Until mother had her stroke.* Caden realized that his visits to Dallas had essentially ended then.

"Anybody home?" Beth called once they were inside.

"Guess Dad's gone out." Caden took a step toward the door. "I'll bring in our suitcases." He turned and looked at Beth. "Unless you'd feel more comfortable at a motel. Things are a little ... unusual right now."

"You're talking about Jean being a part of all this," Beth said.

Caden nodded silently.

"We came to be with your father, and I think our place is here with him."

"I guess you're right. I should be around for Dad." Then Caden muttered something under his breath.

"What was that?"

"Besides, I want to find out what's going on between him and Jean."

"Why do you think anything's going on?" Beth said.

"I don't like the way she's acting, like she's more than just an office nurse." Before anything more was said, Caden heard the garage door open. "Guess Dad's home."

"Why don't you go talk with him?" Beth said, heading up the staircase. "I want to freshen up."

Caden called out, "Dad?"

"I'm headed for my study. Sit down and talk with me."

Caden's father was in the process of taking his usual chair. The drapes were open, and rather than turning to look at his son, Henry stared out the window. His head still turned away, he gestured toward the chair facing him. "Were things at the nursing home about like you expected?"

"Pretty much." Caden didn't like the juxtaposition of the subjects, but there was a question he needed to ask his father, and this was as good a time as any. "Dad, I was surprised when Jean opened the door for us. Honestly, I didn't expect her to be here. I don't want to be rude, but you taught me to be direct. So, is something going on between you and Jean?"

His father was silent for a moment, as though considering the question. Caden had never known him to do anything without careful deliberation. Whereas most surgeons made rapid decisions, his dad took his time. Finally, he turned to look directly at his son. "When your mother had her cerebral hemorrhage, I hardly left her side in the ICU for over a week."

"I know Dad. I was there too."

"Then you remember Jean was in the ICU waiting room with me. She was the one who sent me home to shower, shave, and put on fresh clothes from time to time."

Caden reached up and wiped away the moisture from the corner of his eyes. "I know."

"And you recall that when it was obvious your mother wouldn't wake up tomorrow or the next day—or ever—I encouraged you to go back home. But I stayed with your mother. Eventually, I took a little time to go to the office, but even then, my mind was with Nancy, back there in the hospital. By the time we transferred her to Sunset Rest, I had about reached the breaking point."

Caden responded, just to keep the words coming. "I know Dad."

"That was when I decided I needed someone I could talk to. I certainly couldn't dump all my depression and anger on you. And, unfortunately, I hadn't made any close friends... at least, not close enough for that purpose."

It didn't escape Caden that his father made no mention of talking with his pastor. His mother had always been active in the church, but he remembered his dad tended to shy away from it. Apparently, that hadn't changed. "And you turned to Jean?"

His father touched the breast pocket of his shirt, and Caden realized he was reaching for a cigarette, a habit he'd kicked more than twenty years ago. "Yes. And it helped."

"And this has been going on for... how long? Since Mom's stroke?"

His father looked at the ceiling and seemed to be remembering. "Nancy's been in a vegetative state for over a year. I guess I held out for two or three months before I started unloading on Jean."

"Why did you ask her to be here to meet us? Was it just to cook? Was I supposed to see her play hostess?" He felt a catch in his throat. "Did you want me to see her in this environment, sort of get me used to it?"

The elder Taggart shook his head slowly. "When I knew you were coming, I asked her to prepare something. But if you'll notice, she didn't eat with us. She prepared lunch, then left. Jean wanted us to have some family time together."

"Where did you go while we were gone? Did you go to Jean's?"

"Yes, after you left for the nursing home, I went to Jean's to talk some more. I wanted to see if she thought you were taking this okay." His father leaned forward in his chair. "She thinks the world of you, Caden. I wish you could see that."

Caden took a deep breath. Here came the big question, one he was afraid to ask because of the answer he expected. "So, what's your relationship with her?"

"I don't know how to put this into words, but let's just say that Jean's been the person who's helped me hold it together for the past year or so."

"Has Jean taken Mom's place in your life?" *And is she trying to eventually replace her?*

"I found that talking with her helped me," his father said. "I needed someone to share things with, to bounce stuff off of. She was understanding and supportive." Caden started to speak, but his father held up one finger. "But that's as far as it's gone ... or will go, as long as your mother is alive."

There it was. Jean was someone his father could talk to. Caden was as close as the phone, but his relationship with his father had always been distant. His mother was the one to whom his dad went. When Caden married Beth, she became the confidant he needed. Now Jean was filling that role with his father.

The next statement came out before Caden's internal filter could stop it. "Did you ever think that Mother wouldn't want to live in her present state?"

"Many, many times. Long ago, when we drew up wills, Nancy and I executed advance directives, giving each other the power to withdraw life support. Neither of us wanted to be kept alive when there was no chance of our ever recovering. I had that power for Nancy."

"Dad, I—"

His father shook his head. "I guess I'd better execute another advance directive, so you can do what needs to be done for me."

Caden let that go. He had to follow the path he'd started down. "But, Dad. Did you think about withdrawing life support when the neurosurgeon told you Mom's cerebral hemorrhage wasn't a survivable event?"

"Yes, I thought about it," he said. "But, in retrospect, the neurosurgeon and I were both dragging our feet, hoping for a miracle. Neither of us wanted to be the one to make that final decision. While that was going on, Nancy began breathing on her own. She started to maintain her blood pressure without IV medications. She stabilized while we thought things over. Soon she was staying alive without any artificial means—no life support in that sense. She could survive like that, but it was evident by then she'd never come out of her coma."

"Why didn't you do something?"

"We could have let her starve—withheld water or nourishment. But there was a chance she might still feel things. And I couldn't do that to her." Caden's father wiped a tear from his eye. "The neurosurgeon and I talked about administering what amounted to an overdose of morphine, so Nancy would slip away with no pain. But I couldn't do that either. It might be quicker than starvation, but it amounted to the same thing." He turned his head away from Caden and once more gazed out the window. "It would be murder."

Caden nodded. He wondered if his father realized that what he'd mentioned to his son would also be murder.

As their car pulled away, Beth looked in her side-view mirror and watched the Taggart home grow smaller and smaller. Finally, she turned toward Caden, who was at the wheel. "Are you sure you don't want to stay longer? It's only Saturday afternoon. We've been here for less than a full day."

Caden's eyes never left the road as he replied. "I think it's time to head back home. I talked with Dad. I visited Mom. I did what I needed to do. Now I think we should leave."

"We planned to stay the whole weekend. Does this have anything to do with finding that your father is leaning on Jean a lot?"

He didn't answer for a few minutes. Finally, Caden said, "I don't know. What I do know is this visit confirmed what I already knew—Dad will do what he wants to without my input."

"You mean his medical care?"

"That, of course. But his personal life, as well—Mom's care, Jean's status, his finances, his practice, everything. My father is a willful individual, and he doesn't want advice from me."

Beth shook her head. *His son is pig-headed too. God, help me change that.*

After a few miles, she broke the silence. "Did you talk about how his patients will be cared for when he has to be away from the practice for tests and treatment?"

"That's another area where he and I disagree. Dad hasn't mentioned his problems to his partner yet."

"His absences are bound to have generated questions."

Caden shrugged. "He apparently deflected them. Dad said that, when the time is right, he'll sit down with Dr. Horner and lay it all out."

"But—"

"I get the impression that my dad is playing this pretty close to his vest."

"Did he ask you not to tell anyone?"

"Not in so many words," Caden said. "Of course, he knew I'd tell you. I haven't decided yet whether to tell my partners or the office staff."

"Any more talk of suicide?" Beth asked. "Where does that stand?"

"I tried to talk him out of even considering it, but he wouldn't commit. Like I said, my dad will do what he wants to, and we're not going to change his mind."

Beth waited until she was sure Caden was through talking about the subject. "I'd like to share this with our pastor and ask for his prayers."

She expected a quick response, but instead her husband furrowed his brow and remained silent. A few moments passed before he said, "My first impulse is to say no, but I guess you wouldn't ask if it weren't important to you."

"I think the more people praying for your father, the better. We can keep the number of people who know about this small, but surely we can let Dr. Pearson know." She put her hand on Caden's shoulder. "I know you sometimes think I'm too focused on religion, but right now there are two things that affect the outcome of your dad's case—the medical care he receives, and the prayers offered up on his behalf. And if the diagnosis is carcinoma of the pancreas, medical care can only help so much—sometimes not at all. I think prayer is important."

"I suppose it's okay," Caden said. "I'm sure Dr. Pearson will keep this confidential."

"We can emphasize that when we tell him tomorrow after church."

"We?" Caden turned toward her. "I thought you'd tell him."

"We'll decide who tells him when we see him in the morning," Beth said. She planned for him to accompany her to church this Sunday, and he hadn't argued. It wasn't much of a victory, but it was a victory. And she thought it might be important in the days ahead.

Caden relaxed behind the wheel of the car. They were within a couple of miles of the city limits of Freeman, and he was enjoying watching the last of the fields roll by before farmland gave way to houses and then to shopping centers. That was one of the things both he and Beth enjoyed about living here—it was possible to drive just a few miles outside of town and see pastures with cattle and horses. He wondered how long it would be before they'd be selling their home in the city to move to one a bit farther out, one that would be perfect for their children. That is, if his practice took off and he could afford to make the move. And if they had children.

Caden glanced in the rearview mirror and noted that a black pickup was approaching from the rear. He moved slightly toward the shoulder, just to give the vehicle some extra room if it needed it. When the vehicle passed them, he could see two teenaged boys in the truck, whooping about something. They were just two kids out joyriding, not a care in the world. Caden wished he could go back fifteen years or so and be carefree again.

Beth's yell came at the same time Caden saw what was happening in front of them. The white Lexus in the oncoming lane swerved a couple of times, then gradually but inexorably drifted to the right and off the road. The vehicle hardly slowed as it took down the wire fence around the field before hitting one of the hay bales there. It stopped with the driver leaning over the steering wheel and the motor still racing.

Caden pulled to a stop on the opposite shoulder. "Call 911. We need police and paramedics stat. I'll see what I can do."

He left the car without waiting for Beth to answer. There was not a vehicle in sight in either direction. He sprinted across the highway, went through the opening the wayward vehicle had made in the wire fence, and pushed through ankle-high grass to the car, which was still running, straining against the large cylindrical bale of hay. When Caden opened the left front door of the Lexus, he saw the driver slumped forward and unresponsive. He reached across the man and turned off the ignition.

The driver was a short, stout, older man dressed in a gray pin-striped suit, blue oxford cloth shirt unbuttoned at the neck, and conservative red and blue patterned tie that had been pulled down. His glasses had been knocked askew when he hit the steering wheel. His receding hair was mostly gray. Beside him on the seat sat two well-worn leather briefcases.

Caden saw no bullet wound or similar evidence of causative trauma. He placed two fingers on the driver's neck to feel his carotid pulse. It was faint and slow, but regular, consistent with Caden's initial impression of a heart attack of some type. But making the diagnosis didn't help, because he had no medications to give.

He reached across the driver and undid the seat belt. Then Caden hauled him out of the car, laying him on his back beside the vehicle. He checked the man's pulse again. Faint, but still regular. The respirations were weak. Was his pressure dropping? Caden didn't even have a blood pressure cuff. *I need those paramedics. Now!*

Caden further loosened the man's dress shirt collar and tie, then covered him with a blanket he'd found on the rear seat of the Lexus. He needed an oxygen mask of some type, as well as an IV and medications. Was the patient in shock? Caden started to raise the man's legs but stopped when he thought about the possibility of broken legs. An X-ray would come later, but better not chance it. He was powerless to do more than keep the patient warm.

Beth hurried up. "Help is on its way. Can I do something?"

Caden's reply came through clenched teeth. "Not unless you have oxygen. And maybe some injectable adrenaline or vasopressin."

The man's pulse, when Caden checked it again, seemed to be getting fainter with each passing moment. Then he heard a siren in the distance, growing steadily louder. Help was on the way. The ambulance would have the drugs and oxygen Caden needed to save this patient's life.... he hoped.

Did he wish he'd just driven on by, maybe used his cell phone to report the accident? No, if he'd done that, the driver would probably be dead by the time help reached him. Besides, this was the life's work Caden had chosen. Now he had it, up close and personal.

The vehicle was an MICU, a Mobile Intensive Care Unit. It stopped on the shoulder near where the Lexus had plowed through the fence. The emergency medical technicians hurried up, one carrying a kit with the meds for which Caden had been wishing.

"What have we got?" the one with the kit asked.

"He lost control of his car and ended up here. Probably a cardiac event. I'm a physician, but I didn't have anything with me to treat him."

The EMT nodded, and both he and his partner went straight to work. The next few minutes were a flurry of activity. Caden drew up and administered medications, while the other two men took care of getting an IV started and placing an oxygen mask over the patient's face.

"Can we get an EKG tracing in your MICU?" Caden asked.

The lead attendant nodded.

"Then let's get going."

One of the EMTs ran to the MICU, climbed in, and drove through the damaged fence to stop the ambulance next to the wrecked Lexus. Caden held the back doors open while the two techs loaded the injured man.

Caden followed the stretcher into the back of the MICU. "I'll ride with you. Head for the hospital in Freeman, code three."

"What about your wife?" the lead EMT asked as he climbed behind the wheel.

"She'll drive our car home. Don't worry about her. Let's save this man's life."

5

Beth couldn't recall the last time she and Caden had been gone for any length of time, but she still remembered the routine. Once she'd closed the garage door, she started in the kitchen and went through the house, checking that everything was secure. When she reached the front door, she found it unlocked. Their front door had a double lock, and both were undone. Had they failed to engage the locks? Beth didn't think so.

She left the door unlocked—she might have to make a rapid exit—and hurried to the kitchen, where she armed herself as best she could, choosing the longest knife from her cutlery drawer. Then she went stealthily from room to room, her adrenaline level hitting the top of the meter. She held the knife in one hand, cell phone in the other, with 9-1-1 already dialed, ready to press "call." Finally, satisfied that nothing was missing and that no one was in the house, she backtracked to the front door and engaged both locks. Only then did she return the knife to the kitchen.

Beth started to phone Caden but didn't know how tied up he would be with the emergency case. Should she call the police? Would they send someone to investigate, or was it even worth it? She decided to wait a bit on that. Next, Beth called their neighbor, the widow who'd offered to care for their kitten while they were gone.

"I'm so glad you're back," Mrs. Westwood said. "I think Kitty missed you. I'll bring her right over."

In a few moments, the neighbor was at the door, cuddling the playful tan ball of fur. "Are you sure you don't want the leftover cat food you brought over?"

"No, we have enough. Just leave it and the extra litter box over at your house if you would." Beth knew they might be gone for Henry's funeral at some time in the future. She didn't say it, but she thought it. "Did you happen to see anyone around the house while we were gone?"

"No. Were you expecting someone?"

"Not really. I just found the front door unlocked."

Mrs. Westwood shook her head. "That was probably me. I couldn't find the food you brought over for Kitty, so I used the key you gave me. I guess I neglected to lock the door when I left." She frowned. "Did someone get in? Is there anything missing?"

"No. No harm done, I guess."

She put the kitten down, told Mrs. Westwood thank you again, and double-locked the front door after her. Beth still didn't feel secure, but at least there was an explanation for the unlocked doors. No need to call the police or bother Caden.

It was a couple of hours later when Beth heard the front door open and Caden's voice. "Beth, are you home?"

She could hear a diesel engine pulling away, and assumed the MICU crew had driven her husband home.

"In here." She headed for the kitchen to warm the supper Caden had missed. She was putting the dishes into the oven when he entered the room. Beth turned to exchange hugs and kisses with her husband.

He sniffed the air. "Smells good. Have you already eaten?"

"No, I wanted to wait for you. It will be heated in a few minutes."

Beth poured a glass of iced tea and put it on the kitchen table. Caden sat down and drained half of it before he put it down.

"You look wrung out," Beth said. "Was it a heart attack?"

"Yes. The man—Nolan Sewell is his name, by the way—Mr. Sewell sustained an almost total occlusion of the left anterior descending coronary artery."

"In other words, a heart attack." Beth stirred sweetener into her glass of tea. "How was he when you got to the hospital? When the attendants loaded him into the MICU, it looked like he was barely hanging on."

"He responded to the meds I gave him on the ride. And I was able to monitor him all the way to the ER."

"So, your treatment kept him alive," Beth said.

"It helped, I guess," Caden replied. "The cardiologist on call was Joe Ogle. He saw him in the ER and took over his care. When I left the hospital, they had just finished the angiogram. Sewell needed two stents, but he should pull through."

"When you bless the food, don't forget to pray for your patient."

"He's not really my patient," Caden protested. "I just stayed with him until we got him to the hospital."

"And saved his life," Beth said. "I think it's fair to call him your patient."

"I guess." After a brief blessing—in which Caden included Nolen Sewell and his caregivers—he picked up his fork and began to eat.

Beth decided Caden probably needed to know what had happened with the lock, although it didn't appear to be important. "When I got home, I found the front door unlocked. Mrs. Westwood dropped off Kitty and said she must have left it that way when she came over for more cat food."

"Have you looked around to check?"

"I went through the whole house right after I got home. There's nothing to suggest that anyone has been in here."

"I guess the logical explanation is that Mrs. Westwood is right, and she left the door unlocked," Caden said. He looked through the kitchen doorway and saw the blinking red light on the living room phone. He pointed. "Did you see that?"

"No. I guess I was too preoccupied with the front door being left unlocked."

"Let's see what it is. Probably some spam call." Caden put down his napkin and moved to the living room, where he punched the button to retrieve the message.

It was a short one, delivered by a voice that appeared to have been electronically altered. "Don't believe everything you hear from the DEA agents."

On Sunday morning, Caden pulled his Subaru Outback into a space in the parking lot of the First Community Church of Freeman. He turned off the engine, then looked at Beth. "I still wonder about your finding our front door unlocked. Doesn't that make you feel a bit vulnerable?"

"Yes, but that doesn't necessarily mean someone was in the house. Mrs. Westwood admits she may have left the door unlocked."

Caden unbuckled his seat belt. "I suppose you're right. I looked at the door and didn't see any scratches on the lock plate or gouges on the wood. And I doubt the police would find any meaningful fingerprints."

"Stop worrying about it." Beth climbed from the car. "We won't call the police—mainly because there's nothing to see. We simply need to be cautious for a while."

Inside the church, Caden stopped at a vacant row of pews toward the back. "Let's sit here. I'll take the aisle seat in case I get a call."

After they were seated, Beth leaned over and whispered to her husband. "You aren't on call this weekend. You just like sitting on the aisle."

He felt sheepish when he realized he'd been caught. He figured he accompanied Beth to church less than half the time she went, and when he did he liked to choose a seat on the aisle toward the back of the church. That way, he could stretch his legs from time to time. There were very few seats in this church—or any church for that matter—built to accommodate a six-foot-three man like him. The excuse for his choosing the location apparently hadn't fooled his wife, but this was the first time she'd called him on it.

Caden had been a Christian since making that decision at age twelve. But, like a lot of his generation, as soon as he left home one of the first things he dropped was church attendance. This began when he started his pre-med college work and continued while he was in medical school. His justification was that his time was taken up with his studies. After graduation, Caden's schedule during his surgical residency was intense, so church attendance took a back seat to sleeping in when he could. That didn't change when he and Beth were married, but he vowed it would be different after he entered private practice. He would get back to praying, to reading the Bible, to making God a part of his life—later.

Before his mother had the brain bleed that changed her life and that of her family, she'd gently urged him to get back on track. His answer was always, "I'll do it soon... but not yet." As he thought about it, Caden couldn't recall his father ever saying anything to him about church. That was his mother's thing.

During the offertory prayer Caden found his thoughts drifting. Despite what his medical training told him, he kept hoping the tentative diagnosis of his father's illness would be wrong.

As for his mother, Caden wasn't sure what he wanted to ask God for. She had been comatose for longer than a year, but because she was otherwise in good health, there was no telling how much longer she'd live in a vegetative state. Would death be a blessing for her?

Then it occurred to Caden that it wasn't so much what he wanted as what God decreed. In other words, the phrase he'd heard so many times: "Thy will be done." Now he understood some of the anguish that went with those words—the anguish Jesus felt when he laid down his life, and for that matter, the pain that the Father experienced when He sent his Son to the cross.

Caden stood up at the end of the service. He was about to step into the aisle when Beth touched his sleeve. "We'll wait here until the crowd has thinned before we talk with Dr. Pearson."

"You're still going to tell him about Dad? I'm not certain I feel comfortable doing this," Caden said.

"But I do. The pastor needs to know about the problems you and I are facing—all of them. He'll pray for us, but he might also have some suggestions about what we should do."

"Well, he didn't make things easier for me with today's sermon."

The message had been based on the Ten Commandments, and as Dr. Pearson read the passage from Exodus where they were set forth, Caden's thoughts were centered on two of them. His father had asked for his help if needed to escape suffering by taking his own life. His mother was locked into a vegetative state from which there was no hope of return.

If he did as his dad had hinted, he'd be carrying out his father's wishes by helping him commit suicide. But wasn't that the same as murder? And if Caden somehow decided to do what he'd wondered about on several occasions—to intervene in his mother's situation—would the fact that he might be helping her escape a prison in which she'd been locked for a year mean he was murdering her? And if he did nothing for either of them, would he be failing to honor his parents?

Which one takes precedence? Honor thy father and mother? Or thou shalt do no murder?

The phone rang at three in the morning. By reflex and muscle memory, Caden rolled over and picked up the receiver. Before he could answer, he heard the same electronically altered voice. "Remember what I said about the DEA investigation." The message was followed by a click.

He sat on the side of the bed holding the phone, wondering what these two calls meant. Caden didn't know anything the DEA could use, and he had no intention of talking to the agents more than he had to.

Beth roused from sleep. "Whuh ..."

"Nothing important," Caden said. "Go back to sleep."

He lay wide-eyed for quite a while, but eventually fell into a restless sleep. When he awakened to Beth's gentle nudge, Caden rolled out of bed, but not even the smell of the freshly brewed coffee in the mug she held out to him was enough to get him going. He'd once heard "anxiety" defined as "an unreasonable fear of the unknown." Well, he knew what bothered him, and worrying about it wasn't unreasonable.

He wasn't sure what was the most bothersome—the prospect of the DEA nosing around in his practice, the vague anonymous phone calls about the investigation, the almost certainly lethal diagnosis his father had been given, or the fact that, with his mother in a vegetative state, his father's nurse might be working toward replacing her.

Normally, Caden read through the newspaper as he ate breakfast before Beth. This morning he barely glanced at the headlines. There was the usual mess of name-calling in Washington. Locally, the lead story involved two winos being shot on skid row. Nothing meaningful. Nothing that held his attention. He put the paper aside and tried to down his breakfast.

He managed to eat most of a muffin and drink a glass of orange juice along with a cup of coffee before he headed out. When he reached his office, Caden found that he was the first of the surgeons to arrive. None of the three had surgery scheduled for today, so he'd asked them to meet with him before the day began. Caden planned to explain the presence of the DEA agents. He figured the story he'd come up with was adequate.

As he sat in his office waiting for his colleagues to arrive, he thought back to how his one-man practice had come to include a second and later a third surgeon. When he came to Freeman to get started, Caden felt that sharing space would be good for both him and Ann Russell, who moved here at about the same time from the residency program they both completed.

Ann was a knockout—there was no other way to describe her. Because of her grades and talent, she had her choice of surgical training programs, and she chose the prestigious one at Parkland Hospital in Dallas. It was there she met Caden, who got into that residency on the basis of some excellent recommendations that apparently made up for his rather average medical school grades.

A few months after Caden and Ann opened their practices, Dr. Jim Sparling contacted him about renting the remaining space in his suite. Jim said he'd planned to move from his residency to a faculty position at the Cleveland Clinic, but at the last minute he'd changed his mind and decided on this mid-sized town in north Texas. He said he wanted to be closer to his aging parents, who lived in Fort Worth. When Caden tried to check on Sparling's background, he found that the surgeon's work as a resident was excellent, but he was unable to find out whether Jim ever had an offer from the Cleveland Clinic for a faculty position.

Thus far the arrangement worked reasonably well. They all shared the same suite of offices, but each maintained their own practice. Caden was the man whose name was on the mortgage for the property, while the other two paid him rent and a proportionate amount of the shared expenses.

Ann and Jim arrived within seconds of each other. Caden beckoned them into his office. "Close the door, would you, Jim?" The two took chairs across the desk from Caden.

Ann spoke first. "I hear you had visitors last week. The office staff is curious, and frankly, so am I. Care to enlighten us?"

"That's what I wanted to talk with both of you about. The two men were Dr. Darren Neilson and Dr. Jerry Harwell. Dr. Neilson was an assistant professor at the Wash U medical center, and Dr. Harwell was in private practice in Seattle. They're internal medicine specialists who are thinking about setting up practice here. They were intrigued by our cost-sharing situation and wondered if it would be okay for them to see how our little group functions."

Caden was surprised at how easily the lies flowed and how well they were accepted.

"Are they both going to be looking around?" Ann asked.

"As I understand it, one will concentrate on how our office is set up, while the other checks out things like the hospitals and pharmacies. I don't know exactly how they'll do it but let them have free rein."

"How long will they be here? Do we need to take them out to dinner?" Jim said.

"Not at all. I think they'd prefer to be left alone, so no dinners or anything."

Ann nodded. "Should we feel free to tell the staff what's going on?"

"I intend to let the staff know, but if you two would spread the word that would help. I'm sure the two men want to keep things low-key."

The meeting broke up and the surgeons headed for the door, but when Caden started to follow his colleagues out of his office, Donna was standing in the hallway with the two DEA agents.

There was an awkward silence before Neilson spoke. "I'm sorry. Did we interrupt a conference? We can wait."

"No, we were just heading out." Caden went around the group making introductions, careful to use the titles and histories he'd just manufactured.

Ann spoke first. "Please let us know if there are any questions we can answer." Then she walked away.

Jim nodded at the two men and followed her.

"Want to come into my office for a minute?" Caden said. He'd gotten so involved in the cover story he'd given Ann and Jim that he'd almost forgotten the real reason behind the presence of his visitors. But his first glance at Neilson and Harwell brought him back to reality. Their look was anything but cordial. And he remembered the words of the anonymous phone caller.

Without being asked, the agents took chairs.

"Ready for this?" Neilson said.

"Yes. Here's the cover story I came up with to explain your presence." Caden outlined what he'd told his colleagues that morning. "They seemed to take it okay."

Neilson looked at Harwell, then nodded.

Harwell lowered his voice, even though the door was closed. "My brother-in-law is in orthopedics in Seattle, and I've spent some time in his office, so between what I've picked up there and in conversation around our dinner table, I think I can carry off my role as a private practitioner. I'll look around the office."

"And I'll check out the town, visit the pharmacies and hospitals, that kind of thing," Neilson said. "We'll switch later if we need to."

Caden had no problem with that. What he did have a problem with was how he'd noticed Harwell's eyes follow Ann down the hall when she left. He glanced at the agent's left hand and didn't see a wedding ring. He hoped Harwell's presence in the office wouldn't cause complications.

As the agents rose, Caden said, "By the way, I was wondering why agents from the Dallas field office weren't leading this investigation. It seems strange to send you all down here from Seattle."

Neilson spread his hands, palms-up, in a "What are you going to do?" gesture. "The higher-ups wanted unfamiliar faces, so they sent us."

"Exactly what are you looking for?" Caden asked.

Neilson shrugged. "Just let us do our thing. If we have questions, we'll come to you—unless what we find implicates you."

6

When Beth heard Caden's car stop in the driveway that night, she dried her hands on her apron and moved toward the front door to meet her husband. Like many of the families in the community, their garage had gradually been taken over by things for which they had no immediate need but didn't want to throw away. They'd tried to keep at least half of the space clear for their Subaru Outback, but the older car—the Ford Fusion—sat outside. For now, Caden drove the Ford. The Subaru was newer and reserved for trips ... and Beth's use, especially whenever their family grew.

Caden barely had time to toss down his backpack, which he'd carried since his days in med school, before Beth gave him a kiss and hug. Kitty twined around his ankles, but Caden's attention was on his wife. When they pulled apart, she said, "Tell me about it. How did the meeting with the DEA agents go?"

He moved to the living room and eased down onto the sofa. When Beth had assumed her usual position beside him, he said, "Sort of a mixed bag, I guess. The agents switched the roles I'd envisioned for them, with

Harwell—he's the younger one—hanging around the office. Because he's familiar with an office routine, he felt like he could carry off the role better than Neilson, who'll be checking out pharmacies, hospitals, all that stuff."

"Did your colleagues and the staff seem to buy your story?"

"Yeah, they did. But I didn't like the way Harwell looked at Ann Russell when they met."

Beth frowned. "I thought Ann was like the flower—you know, 'touch me not.'"

"She's always been that way in the past, but I hope Harwell doesn't make a play for her. If he gets too close to her, or to any of the staff, he may blow his cover."

"You're not jealous, are you? Wish your wife were a good-looking blonde instead of someone drab like me?" Beth said it in a joking tone, but underneath was a bit of truth. When she was working as a nurse, she got her share of compliments from male doctors about her brunette good looks and slim figure. Did she miss them? She wasn't sure.

Caden kissed the tip of her nose. "The first time I saw you, I knew you were the only woman for me, and that hasn't changed. I just hope Harwell doesn't foul up this thing. I want the DEA investigation to be over."

"But what if they find some connection to you?"

"Someone may be using my name and DEA number, but unless the agents find evidence that I was directly involved, I think I'm in the clear."

Beth stopped and sniffed, then rose from her seat on the sofa. "Come on to the kitchen and help me. I'm glad you like the wife you have, but it's probably best if I don't put a burnt offering in front of you this evening."

Caden had only one consultation request at the hospital on Tuesday morning, one that was reasonably easy. While he was there, he decided he'd look in on Nolan Sewell, the patient he'd helped treat for a heart attack. He doubted that Sewell had already been discharged, and when Caden inquired at the information desk, he was told that Mr. Sewell had gone from the CCU to a private room.

When Caden entered Sewell's room, he found the patient lying quietly in bed, a tube delivering oxygen into his nostrils, an IV running into his left arm. The monitor at the head of the bed showed vital signs within the normal range.

A man about Caden's age sat at the bedside. He wore a dark blue suit and a white dress shirt with a conservative tie. Horn-rimmed glasses sat low on his nose. He read out loud from a multi-page document, occasionally stopping to add a comment.

When the visitor in the chair realized Caden was standing in the doorway, he turned and half-stood. "Do I need to get out of the way? Are you here to examine my father?"

"No," Caden said. "I'm not officially his doctor. I'm Dr. Taggart. I pulled your father out of his car and rode with him in the ambulance to the hospital." He took a tentative step inside the room. "I just wanted to check on him, but I see I'm interrupting. I'll leave you folks."

The younger man popped out of his chair and covered the distance to Caden in three long strides. He extended his hand. "I'm Mel Sewell. My dad and I were wondering how we'd get in touch with the man who saved his life. And here you are."

"Doctor," the man on the bed said in a quiet voice. "Come here and let me thank you."

"No thanks necessary," Caden said. "I'm just glad you're okay." He approached the elder Sewell and took the offered hand.

"I'm not well, although they tell me I will be. But I'm okay enough to realize that I've been working too hard." The man released Caden's hand. "I've already told Mel that I need to pull back. Soon the law firm of Sewell and Sewell will rest squarely on his shoulders, and I'll simply be a name on a letterhead."

Caden was a bit embarrassed. He'd obviously walked in on a family conversation. "I'll leave you two to continue your conversation." He pulled two cards from his wallet. He gave one to Mel Sewell and laid the other on Nolan Sewell's bedside table. "Let me know if I can help in the future."

Mel Sewell pulled a pigskin card case from the inside pocket of his suit. He uncapped a gold pen and wrote on the back of one of the cards, then handed it to Caden. "That's the card for the law firm. I've written the number of my cell phone on the back. Call me if I can ever help you with anything."

Caden took the card and put it in his wallet. He took his leave of the two men, happy that he'd been able to save Nolan Sewell's life, yet a bit embarrassed at their reaction to his actions. He'd just done what he felt he should do under the circumstances.

He glanced at his watch and found that he had time to drop by the surgeons' lounge. Maybe there'd be one of his colleagues there who wanted to talk. There often was, but this time the room was empty.

Caden drew a cup of what he'd already decided was the world's worst coffee, added cream and sugar to mask the bitterness, and sipped. How could coffee that had been made only an hour or so earlier taste like it had sat in the urn overnight? He decided that was one of the mysteries he'd never solve…that and why his father had been diagnosed with cancer. The world wasn't fair. Just let it go at that.

As he was halfway through his cup of coffee, Dr. Ann Russell came through the door. She headed for the coffee urn, where she stood staring at it for a few moments. Then she shrugged, took a Styrofoam cup, and half-filled it.

"Tough case this morning?" Caden said. "Sit down and tell me about it."

"Emergency case last night. Woman with a ruptured aortic aneurysm."

"I'm surprised you didn't call me to assist."

"No time," she said. "Jim Sparling had just finished an emergency appendectomy, so I asked him to help me. I did most of the work."

"When's the last ruptured aneurysm you did?"

"Probably not since residency, but I guess it's sort of like riding a bike. If I'd sent the patient to a specialist in Dallas, she wouldn't have made it. She was literally bleeding to death internally. This way, I managed to save her." She took a sip from her cup, made a face, and tossed it untouched into a nearby wastebasket. "Will you look in on her tonight?"

"Sure." Caden wrote down the patient's name and room number.

"Right now, I'm off for home. It was a long—and sleepless—night. I guess I should have listened to Dr. Barfield when he tried to talk me into psychiatry."

"Let's face it," Caden said. "You wouldn't be happy doing anything else."

Ann nodded. "You're right. We all choose the brand of misery that makes us happiest, if that makes any sense at all." And with that, she headed for the women's dressing room.

Caden took a sip of his heavily doctored coffee, then followed his colleague's lead and tossed the partially filled cup in the trash. Ann was right. When he determined he'd practice general surgery, Caden knew he was in for some emergency cases that would keep him up all night, situations that would challenge his skills, even some heart-wrenching scenarios. But this was the path he'd set out on, and he wouldn't trade.

We all choose the brand of misery that makes us happiest. And he'd chosen this particular brand of misery. He'd do his best for his patients and hope those caring for his father would do the same thing. As he headed toward the door, his shoulders were a little less slumped. *Thanks, Ann. I needed that.*

The tech tapped on the door and entered the room where Henry Taggart sat. "You've taken all the contrast solution?"

"Of course," Henry said. "I took it quite a while ago. Then I sat around for what seemed like forever, wearing a gown that left my back end exposed, waiting for you to get things going." His emotions vacillated between resentment at being treated like any other patient and anger that proliferation of some random cells inside his belly made the procedure necessary.

The technician was apparently no stranger to patients—even medical professionals—who vented their emotions while undergoing procedures like this. Henry's comments didn't elicit a reply from the tech. Instead, he asked, "Now what kind of music do you want to listen to while we do this?"

"Can't I just lie quietly and relax without having music blaring in my ears?"

He knew why he was being offered earphones and piped-in music. The CAT scan involved a lot of noise and required the patient to lie still for half an hour or so. Something to keep the mind (and brain) occupied was undoubtedly a good idea. The truth of the matter was that he simply didn't want to be here in the first place.

Henry took a calming breath. "Do you have something sort of soothing?" he asked before the technician could repeat the question. He just wanted to get the test over with.

After they settled on easy listening instrumentals, Henry adjusted the padded headset over his ears and took his place on the slab-like bed. He half-listened to the technician's explanation of what was about to happen. So far as he was concerned, what he planned to do was lie there and let the tech take over.

He had turned down the suggestion of his oncologist that he take Valium to pre-medicate himself before the test. Lying still for thirty minutes could seem like an eternity, but Henry decided he would go through this experience without pharmaceutical help. In his surgical practice, he couldn't begin to count the number of times he'd ordered this same test or a variant of it, aware to some extent of the mental and emotional trauma associated with it but writing it off as necessary. Now Henry was getting the opportunity to experience it firsthand. He'd generally offered a pill to help calm his patients, but perversely he declined one for himself.

After the test had gone on for an interminable length of time, the technician's voice came through his earphones. "About five more minutes. Hang in there." It seemed more like thirty, but finally the electronic voice in his ear said, "All done." Henry breathed a sigh of relief. He'd never again subject a patient to this ordeal without some words of encouragement—and a strong suggestion that they avail themselves of sedation during the experience.

"What do the images look like?" Henry asked after he was dressed again.

"The radiologist will review them and contact your physician," the technician said in a tone that indicated he'd said this before.

"Look, I'm a doctor," Henry said. "Why can't I look at the images?"

"I just check them to make sure they're technically adequate. The radiologist will review them—"

"I know. 'And contact my physician.' Thanks anyway."

On Wednesday afternoon, Henry was fully clothed as he sat in Dr. Gershwin's private office. That was an improvement over his first meeting with the oncologist, when he sat on the table in an exam room, trying unsuccessfully to cover himself with a paper exam gown. Nevertheless, Henry was still nervous. He was usually on the other side of the desk in these situations. This time—despite his three decades of experience as a surgeon—someone else was in control of what would happen next.

He knew as well as any doctor the steps to work up a patient with a presumptive diagnosis of pancreatic carcinoma. Henry could recite the protocol in his sleep. And if that work-up confirmed the diagnosis, he was familiar with the therapeutic options available. Unfortunately, he also knew—and what he still had trouble getting his mind around—was the prognosis that accompanied this diagnosis. Surely it couldn't be happening to him. Patients had this condition. Patients, but not Dr. Henry Taggart.

In treating cancer, doctors talked about what they called "five-year survival." Henry had looked up the figures recently to confirm them for pancreatic cancer. Only about 20 percent of patients survived for one year after diagnosis. The number that lived for five years was even more dismal.

In a long surgical career, Henry had made this diagnosis himself less than a dozen times, and in each instance, he'd referred the patient to a nearby medical center where all types of treatment were available. Truth be told, he hadn't followed those patients to see what their life was like toward the end. As best he could tell from the reading he'd done, it wasn't pleasant. Henry had almost fully made up his mind that he wouldn't reach that stage. He just hoped Caden would help him, if and when it came to that.

"Sorry to keep you waiting," Dr. Gershwin said as he hurried in and took a seat behind his desk. He shrugged, and Henry heard the crackle of starched fabric as the crisp white coat settled on Gershwin's shoulders.

Henry noted that the doctor didn't offer to shake hands. *Already building the wall that changes me from colleague to patient. I guess I'd better get used to that.*

The consultant leaned forward and said, "I've reviewed your CT scan—"

"I tried to look at it myself," Henry said. "The technician said he couldn't let me."

Gershwin shrugged it off. "Rules of the medical center. Anyway, the main thing it tells me is that you have a widened duodenal C-loop, probably due to pancreatic carcinoma, but there's no evidence that it has spread. In other words, your case is amenable to treatment. So…"

Henry nodded.

"I think we proceed with a laparoscopic ultrasound. If we can get a decent needle biopsy that way, we'll have a good idea of where we stand. Then we decide what to do next."

Although Henry was prepared for this—actually, was anxious for the biopsy—he found himself enveloped in a cold sweat. Soon he could have tissue confirmation of the presence of a malignancy growing in his body. At that point, it would go from a clinical scenario to a reality. He was playing host to a tumor that would eventually kill him.

"I'm sorry," Henry said. "I missed that last part. What did you say?"

"I was asking about scheduling the procedure. As you know, this will be purely endoscopic—no real surgery," Gershwin said. "The anesthesiologist will give you something IV, and you probably won't remember a thing. You'll need someone to drive you home though."

Gershwin found the calendar on his desk and pulled it toward him. "I presume you'll want us to do this as quickly as possible."

No, I want this to just go away. Henry swallowed hard. The biopsy would make a likelihood a certainty. He'd no longer carry a diagnosis of suspected pancreatic cancer. It would be proven. Then what would it be? Surgery, chemotherapy, radiation, a gradual dwindling away until he eventually died? Or would he end his life on his own terms?

He tried to put eagerness in his voice and failed. "Sure. The sooner the better."

"*Do you think anyone suspects what's going on?*"

"*Not that I can tell. What have you accomplished so far?*"

"*I've begun to close some of the open loopholes.*"

"*Is that all you're going to be doing?*"

"*No. The false prescriptions have all been concentrated in one area of the city. That means just a few pharmacies. I'll follow up on those as I can.*"

"*You mean buy off the pharmacists?*"

"*That or terminate them. You know. Make it look like a drug addict robbed them.*"

There was silence for a moment on the other end of the line. "*What about patient charts?*"

"*I think I know how to deal with that.*"

"*Let me know if I can help.*"

"*I will. Maybe we can get this taken care of without making too much of a mess.*"

"*Or drawing too much attention.*"

7

Caden sat at his desk on Wednesday afternoon. Across from him were the two agents, Neilson and Harwell. Neilson wore a suit, while Harwell wore a white lab coat over his dress shirt and tie. Caden could read the name embroidered on the breast pocket: Caden Taggart, MD. He wondered if Harwell had chosen that particular white coat because it fit him, or because it was his idea of rubbing it in. Maybe both.

"You men have been working for a couple of days," Caden said. "I know better than to ask what you've found, but can you at least tell me how much longer you plan to be in and out of my office?"

"We should be through here in another day or two." Neilson nodded at the other agent. "We need to discuss with each other what we've learned, fill in some blanks, and then we'll be ready to bring this to an end."

"And when do I know what you've found?"

"Sorry. We can't talk about an ongoing investigation," Neilson said.

Caden took a deep breath, but it didn't help. These men were holding his participation, at least the use of his name and number, over his head. Between what was going on with his father and not knowing what the agents were going to recommend, especially in view of the two anonymous messages he'd received about the DEA investigators, he was finding it difficult to keep his cool.

"I think I'd better get a lawyer. Not because I've done anything wrong, but because I've heard enough stories of innocent people caught up in the wide net you folks spread."

"Look, Dr. Taggart—"

"No, you look." Caden's vocal level was rising, but he didn't care. "I've been nothing but cooperative, and all I get in return is silence. I think I'm going to protect my rights by engaging an attorney. I should have done it earlier, but that's old history. I'm doing it now." He stood up. "Until that time, I'm not going to talk further with you."

The agents looked at each other, nodded at Caden, and left his office.

He pulled from his wallet the card with the cell number of Melvin Sewell. The attorney had said to give him a call if he could ever do anything for the doctor. Well, Caden had decided that he needed an attorney protecting his rights. He laid the card on his desk, pulled his phone toward him, and started dialing.

It was late on Wednesday. Other than the security lights that remained on all night, only one other room in the suite of offices belonging to Doctors Henry Taggart and Claude Horner was lit. The illumination, such as it was, came from the desk lamp in Dr. Taggart's office.

Henry sat behind his desk, the door to his office closed, poring over the printed pages before him. Periodically, he paused to make a notation on the legal pad by his right elbow. He turned page after page of the thick documents, trying to decipher the language and translate it into understandable English. Mainly he wanted to see how it applied to his own situation.

Suddenly, a tap on the door made Henry look up. Before there was time for him to react, it opened slowly to reveal his partner standing there. Claude had a questioning expression on his moon face. He was about the same age as Henry, but unlike his partner, who was tall and a bit lean, Claude Horner was short and chunky. His collar was loosened, and his tie hung at half-mast. His partially gray hair was swept back except for a few unruly strands that defied control.

"Oh!" Claude said. "I wondered why the light was on."

Henry shoved all the papers into his top desk drawer. "I came back after my appointment . . . after I finished this afternoon. I wanted to go over some documents." He stared at Claude. His words were benign, but the tone was a bit accusatory. "What are you doing here?"

"I left my briefcase somewhere. It's not in my office so I decided to look here."

Henry hadn't heard anyone moving around, and no light shone in the hallway behind Claude. His partner's story didn't ring true, but he chose to ignore it. "I haven't seen it, but I'll keep an eye out for it."

The two men were silent for what seemed like an eternity. Finally, Claude gave a short nod. "Thanks. I'll let myself out." He started toward the door, then paused and turned back. "I don't suppose you're ready to tell me where you were this afternoon."

Henry shook his head. "Personal business. Right now, that's all I want to say."

Claude nodded and left, closing the door behind him.

Henry waited at his desk until he heard a car door slam, followed by the sound of a car starting and driving away. When he was satisfied that his partner had left, he opened the desk drawer, removed the papers, and resumed his study of them.

He was looking for the answer to a question—one that would help determine the course of his life, and for that matter, the duration of it.

Caden sat in his recliner in the living room of his home. The TV set was tuned to some sitcom, but he wasn't paying a lot of attention to it. His mind was on his conversation with Mel Sewell earlier today. The lawyer hadn't seemed to mind getting a call when he was about to leave his office, not even when he heard what Caden wanted.

"Have the DEA agents told you what you can and can't reveal about their investigation?" Sewell had asked.

"Not really. I suppose it was just something I assumed."

"What have you done up to this point?"

"I gave my staff and colleagues a cover story to explain the agents' presence. Other than that, nothing."

"Did you think about engaging an attorney?"

"When I asked initially if I needed a lawyer, the senior man didn't really encourage me. He talked about 'keeping it simple.' But today I decided that maybe I'd better engage one." Caden gave a half-chuckle, more apologetic than expressing mirth. "Can you give me a name?"

"Sure. Mel Sewell. Experienced attorney with a great reputation. I'd trust him with my life."

"I didn't call to trade on our history," Caden said. "I just—"

"Look. If you're certain you've done nothing wrong, this will probably consist of no more than a conference, maybe a couple of phone calls. I'll be glad to help you, if you'll let me."

Caden thought about his bank balance—adequate but not unlimited. "What kind of retainer will you need?"

"Mail me a check for a dollar. That establishes a lawyer-client relationship and makes everything we talk about privileged."

"That's ... that's very kind of you."

"You essentially saved my father's life and never sent a bill," Sewell said. "I'm happy to help out. Now get that check to me, and then feel free to let the agents know that future conferences with you will have to include me."

Caden's reverie was interrupted by Beth's appearance in the doorway.

"Penny for your thoughts."

He looked up, startled by her sudden appearance. "I ... I was just watching this TV program."

Beth switched the TV off. "I doubt it. You probably couldn't even tell me what the program was. What's on your mind?"

"I'm sort of ashamed that I let it go this long." He related to her his last conversation with the DEA agents, and then his call to an attorney. "I don't think I'm in any trouble, but I'll feel better with someone protecting my interest through all this."

Before Beth could respond, the landline rang. Since she was still standing, she walked over and answered it. She spoke a few words, then handed the phone to Caden without comment.

"Hello?"

Henry's voice was as calm as though he was relaying a weather report. "Son, I wanted to let you know that I'll have the biopsy on Friday. I'll call you when the pathology report comes back."

"Beth and I can be there—"

"Jean is going to drive me. No need for you to come."

After a bit more conversation, Henry ended the call. Beth looked at him with eyebrows raised, and Caden told her what his dad had called about.

"Do you want to be there?" she asked.

"Yes, I'd like to be with my dad, but he said Jean would drive him to and from the procedure."

Beth nodded. "And you hate it that Jean is going to be with him and you won't. Tell you what. Do you have the home number of your receptionist?"

"Yes, both for Donna and Mona."

"Call one of them. If you can't get in touch with either one, call Rose. Tell her something has come up and you need to be out tomorrow and maybe Friday."

"I can't do that."

"You do it all the time when you have an emergency case. Do you have any surgery the next couple of days? Any consults to see?"

Caden shook his head. "No."

"What about emergency calls?"

"Jim Sparling would cover for me," Caden said. "He's always happy to get a few extra patients."

"So, you can be gone. I'll phone Jean and let her know we'll be there but ask her not to tell Henry. We can stay at a motel in Dallas. When it's over, we'll show up at his house. Trust me, he'll be glad you're there."

"But the DEA …"

"You said the agents weren't thrilled that you're engaging an attorney. Let them stew while you're gone."

"I—"

"We're going. Your father will fuss, but eventually he'll be happy at your presence."

When Caden awoke on Thursday morning, it took him a minute to orient himself to unfamiliar surroundings. Then, little by little, he remembered—the drive yesterday evening; the burger, fries and malt consumed in the car; the problems finding the motel despite directions from his GPS. By the time they'd unpacked their necessities, he and Beth were ready to fall into bed. After that, his sleep was so deep it rivaled general anesthesia. Maybe that was why he was still sort of groggy.

He squinted at the bedside clock and realized that he and Beth needed to get downstairs or they'd miss the buffet breakfast offered by the motel. He felt ravenous, and he wanted about a gallon of coffee to get started. He reached over to shake his wife awake but found her side of the bed empty.

He got up and padded into the next room, grateful that Beth had made their reservation at this all-suites motel, so they'd have a bit more space. She was up and dressed, seated at the desk with their laptop computer open in front of her.

"I guess I slept later than I intended," he said. Then, noticing the cup in front of Beth, he said, "Have you already been downstairs?"

She shook her head and pointed to the coffee maker in the tiny kitchenette area. "There's another cupful in the pot on the counter. That should hold you while you get dressed." Beth glanced at her watch. "If you don't get bogged down, we'll still make it to the breakfast area in time to eat here."

"And if we don't, I vaguely recall passing a couple of fast food restaurants last night." Caden poured the remaining coffee from the pot into a mug and took a long sip.

"I'll make another potful if you need it," Beth said. "Now get going."

As Caden was about to start shaving, he heard his cell phone ringing. He started toward the bedroom to answer but stopped when he heard Beth pick it up. He could hear her voice, although he couldn't discern the words. Well, whatever it was, she'd let him know.

He'd just finished lathering his face when she appeared in the doorway. When Caden saw her face in the mirror, he could tell something was wrong. He turned back to her and said, "What's going on?"

"That was Jean."

His father's procedure wasn't due to start for another hour. *Had something come up? What? Is there a problem with Dad?* "Have they done the endoscopy already?"

"No. The procedure has been cancelled."

"I don't understand."

"Jean went by to pick up Henry this morning, and she found him just putting down the phone. The nursing home had called him." Beth covered the distance between the two of them in a few strides. Heedless of the lather covering his jaw and cheeks, she grabbed Caden and pulled him toward her. Her head buried on his shoulder, she said in a soft voice, "Oh, Honey. They found your mother dead this morning."

Beth stood with Caden outside the Sunset Rest Nursing Home. Neither of them said a word, but as they moved up the walk he reached for her hand. At the front desk, he said, "Dr. Caden Taggart. I believe my mother..." He couldn't finish.

The receptionist responded in a hushed voice, "I'm so sorry for your loss, Dr. Taggart. Your father and his friend are in the room with your mother now." She pointed down the hall. "Last door on the left, number seventeen."

Because she was looking for it, Beth noted that Caden's shoulders momentarily slumped a bit when the receptionist indicated his father hadn't come alone. From her standpoint, Beth was glad that Jean was here. She could provide a shoulder on which Henry could lean—and cry, if need be—the same function Beth saw herself filling.

Although Caden's mother—at least, as he knew her—had been lost to him for over a year, today's events closed the door totally and completely. That was a shock, Beth knew. The fact that there was another woman standing beside his father made the moment even harder for Caden.

When they reached the closed door of number seventeen, Caden let go of Beth's hand and tapped gently. There was a murmur from inside the room—a woman's voice. Beth couldn't make out what was said, but apparently

Caden either took it to be permission or decided to enter anyway.

He drew a deep breath, opened the door, and stepped inside. Nancy was laid out with the sheet pulled to her chin. The tubes for feeding and urinary drainage had been removed. Other than the closure of her eyes, Nancy looked very much the same as when Beth and Caden had last seen her—mannequin-like and unmoving. Only her pallor and the absence of respiration gave an indication that she was now dead.

Henry stood immobile at Nancy's bedside, one hand barely touching the sheet that covered her body. Jean turned to Caden and Beth and said in a soft voice, "I'm so glad you're here."

Caden moved to his father's side and put one arm around him. Henry recognized his son's presence with a nod but said nothing. He continued to stare down at the body of his wife.

Beth motioned Jean toward her. When they were close enough to put their heads together, she whispered, "What happened?"

"I don't know," Jean said quietly. "The administrator called Henry just as he was getting ready to leave for his biopsy. Apparently, the last time the night nurse saw Nancy was around 4:00 a.m. Then, when they went in later to check on her, they found her ... they ..." She shook her head.

Henry glanced at his son. "I'm not sure how you got here so fast, but I'm glad."

Caden squeezed his father's shoulder, then gazed down at the body of his mother.

They stood in silence for several minutes before Henry, without looking up, said, "After you've had enough time with your mother, I'll ask the administrator or head nurse to notify the funeral home to pick up her body. The doctor who's been looking in on her since she was transferred here will sign the death certificate."

"What will happen then?" Caden asked in a low voice. He couldn't force himself to say the words, but Henry would know what his son really wanted to know.

"Your mother and I talked about this long before her stroke. At that time, she wanted to be an organ donor, but I don't think that's an option any more, given her status. She'll be cremated, and I'll take care of disposing of her ashes." He turned his head and stifled a sob.

"Do you want me to help you make arrangements?"

Henry shook his head. "No, I can do that. And as for her funeral, she discussed it with our pastor even before … before her stroke. The memorial service is already planned." He took a deep breath. "I haven't even thought about mine, of course. I guess I should."

"Mom was a Christian, wasn't she?"

"Oh, yes. She made that decision when she was a little girl. I suppose that's one reason she never feared death. I, on the other hand …"

Caden looked over at his father. "Dad—"

"I'll be okay," Henry said. "Let me call our pastor. He'll need to know about this." He turned toward the door. As he and Jean left the room, he said in a low voice, "Besides, I think I need to talk with him about myself."

Beth moved up to stand beside Caden. He reached down and touched his dead mother's face. His lips were moving, but no words came forth. She waited for tears to start, but Caden's eyes remained dry. Finally, he bowed his head. He stood that way for what Beth judged to be a minute or more.

When he looked up, she said, "She's better off now. I know it's hard, but we knew this was coming. We just didn't expect it right now."

Caden shook his head. Then he did something that surprised Beth. Gently, he raised both his mother's eyelids and bent closer to her body. After a few seconds, he closed the corpse's eyes. Then he brushed his lips across her forehead and stepped back.

Beth frowned at this behavior but didn't say anything.

After a moment more, Caden turned and squared his shoulders. "I need to talk with my dad. I'm not sure Mother died a natural death. Someone may have murdered her."

8

Caden had never been in this room, but he'd been in ones like it at various times in the past. Every hospital where he worked, from medical school through residency and on to private practice, had a room like this— sometimes more than one of them.

This room was subtly lit by low-wattage bulbs in table lamps sitting opposite each other, with a sofa in between. The coffee table in front of the sofa bore a Gideon Bible and a box of facial tissues. Upholstered side chairs, their coverings a match for the sofa, sat along the wall. A few artificial flowers, a scrawny ficus tree, and a couple of pictures on the wall completed the decor.

This was the room where a staff member broke the bad news to the family. The social worker gathered everyone here to discuss the options available for hospice care. The doctor or health care worker revealed how the elderly patient had fallen and suffered a broken hip that would require transfer to a nearby hospital. And, in this situation, two men sat together and made their final decisions after the death of a loved one.

Caden realized that when he was younger he had looked to his father and mother for guidance in tough situations.

But his mother had been unable to give counsel for a year or so. Now, rather than Caden seeking the advice of his father, it was up to him to guide his dad, to convince him there was only one right course of action—right but unpleasant.

"Dad, I'm pretty sure there were petechial hemorrhages in Mom's conjunctiva. That means she was choked or smothered. We have to request an autopsy."

"You looked at her eyes for a second or two and think you saw them? I think you're wrong," his father said. "Why can't we let your mother rest in peace?"

"Dad, if I'm wrong, we've held up the process of cremation a day or two at most. And no one need ever know. But if I'm right—"

There was an air of finality to his father's answer. "No. When I was on pathology, I saw bodies of people who'd died of asphyxiation. I'm familiar with those tiny red areas, petechial hemorrhages, in the whites of the eyes. And I don't think your mother had them."

"If you're sure …"

"No autopsy. It's my decision." His father raised his eyes to look directly at his son. "I realize this is hard for you to accept, but you have to let it go."

Caden shook his head. In his mind, it was clear that Jean might have done this. She was a nurse, and she probably wouldn't have any problem slipping in and smothering Nancy Taggart. Either his father couldn't see the obvious advantage to Jean if his mother was out of the way, or he simply turned a blind eye to it.

If his father, as next of kin, wouldn't authorize an autopsy, Caden toyed with the idea of contacting the police. But would that help? Would they order a medico-legal autopsy? There was nothing to hang their hat on but

Caden's suspicions. His father was already digging in his heels. For Caden to pursue the matter might cause a rift between them that would never heal. Then he'd be left with no parents. At least he still had one right now.

"Let's put this behind us and move on. Your mother would want that."

His father clapped him on the shoulder, then rose and turned toward the door. "I need to get in touch with the funeral home. I'll see you at the house."

I'll be there for a while, but I'm not certain I'll stay. I don't know if I can.

When Caden said he didn't want to move from the motel into his parents' home today, Beth didn't try to change his mind. The reason he gave her was that he needed some alone time to process his grief. She figured the real reason was that Jean would be at Henry's house quite a bit during the next few days, providing support for him and acting as hostess for the many people who'd be coming by. Apparently, this was something Caden didn't want to face right now. He needed a place to retreat, and the motel would provide that. As for her feelings, she'd put them aside for now. Her main job was to be at her husband's side through everything she knew would follow.

As they drove away from Sunset Rest, she gave Caden adequate opportunity to talk if he wished, but he remained tight-lipped. Apparently, if Beth wanted to converse, it would be up to her to start. Finally, when they'd gone about three blocks, she began. "You and your father were together in the family room for a long time."

Caden sighed. "I tried to convince Dad to request an autopsy on Mom."

"Why?"

"I think someone murdered her."

"What?"

Beth listened in disbelief as Caden told of seeing tiny red spots in the whites of his mother's eyes. "So those are evidence of smothering?"

"Smothering, strangulation, anything that cuts off the air. The individual struggles for breath, it increases the pressure in those tiny vessels in the eyes until they break, and results in red spots that we call petechial hemorrhages."

"Who would do such a thing?" Beth asked. She thought she knew where Caden was going with this but wanted to give him a chance to say it.

"We both know of one possibility, although I can't convince Dad of it."

Beth knew Caden was referring to Jean. She didn't think that was the case, but perhaps now was not the time to try convincing her husband.

Caden steered around a slower-moving car, then stayed in the right lane for the turn that was coming up.

After a few more minutes of silence, Beth spoke up again. "Shouldn't I call my family and let them know of Nancy's death? They're going to want to be here for the service."

Caden turned in to the motel and found a parking place. "I guess so. Tell your folks Mom is dead, and you'll call back when we know the arrangements. And we need to adjust my schedule. I told the office I'd be gone today, but now I don't know…" He closed his eyes and took several deep breaths. "I can't handle this. Would you make those calls? I don't really want to talk with anyone."

"Of course." Beth looked at her watch. "You know, it's almost one o'clock. Why don't you get something to eat? I'll join you in the coffee shop when I've made the calls."

"I'm not really hungry."

"I know, but you've got to keep up your strength."

Henry Taggart sat alone in his darkened den, the drapes drawn as though by doing so he could shut out the world and ignore the events of the past few hours. In response to Jean's offer to help, he'd asked her to handle anyone who called or came to the door. For now, he needed solitude.

Although Nancy had put it together years ago, Henry knew that the ultimate responsibility for her memorial service rested with him. He'd listen to any suggestions Caden and Beth made, of course. Jean had offered to be involved, but somehow that didn't feel right. Right now, though, Henry didn't want to make any decisions. He wanted to sit here in the dark and let his thoughts wander.

The rupture of a tiny blood vessel inside his wife's skull started the whole process. Neither he nor Nancy had any idea the aneurysm, the weak spot in one of the vessels feeding the brain, was even there. Could it have been treated? Would surgery beforehand have been effective? *It doesn't matter. Nothing matters now. Nancy is dead.*

Why did Caden think his mother was murdered? Henry thought he knew, and it grieved him. Nancy hadn't been sentient for over a year, and Henry had let Jean into his life to fill the void. She was someone to talk with, someone to share decisions with. But his son resented her.

Henry didn't think there were any subconjunctival hemorrhages in Nancy's eyes. That sign might be diagnostic on TV shows, but he knew better. Even if they were there and he got the police involved, it wouldn't bring his wife back. No, she was better off. They were all better off, so just let it be.

Henry had no concept of the passage of time. He could have been sitting there for half an hour or half a day when he was roused from his reverie by a voice he recognized.

"Dad?" Henry looked up and nodded. "Turn on the lights, Caden. I've just been sitting here in the dark."

"Thinking?"

"Sort of."

Caden turned on the table lamp that stood beside his father's chair. He sat down opposite Henry. "I'm sorry to leave you alone for a while. I had to—"

"Don't worry about it," Henry said. "I wanted some solitude, too."

"We won't go into the autopsy thing—I respect your wishes on that—but I wish you'd answer one question," Caden said. "Who would want Mom dead?"

Henry bowed his head. "You've heard the expression, 'Didn't have an enemy in the world?' That was your mother."

"If it wasn't personal, then how about money? What about insurance on her?"

"When she had her stroke, I cashed in her policies except for one that will just about cover her funeral expenses," Henry said. "I can't see any monetary benefit from her … from her death."

"Nothing else?"

"No," Henry said. "And by the way, my policy that names you as beneficiary? It's paid up, and I don't plan to change it. You just won't have to worry about taking care of your mother with the proceeds. Use it however you want—maybe establish a scholarship that will help support residents where you and I trained."

"We won't worry about that right now," Caden said. "Dad, when will you reschedule your procedure with Dr. Gershwin?"

"Does it matter?" Henry said. He saw Caden was about to say something, so he held up his hand to stop him. "Let me get past your mother's funeral. I don't want to do anything about my own problems right now."

"But—"

"Think about it. If the biopsy shows this is all an anomaly, and I don't have pancreatic carcinoma, it doesn't matter if we put it off for a bit. And if the biopsy is positive . . . well, I don't guess a few more days makes any difference in that case, either."

Besides that, if the biopsy is positive, I'm not sure I want the slow death pancreatic cancer could bring. And if I die by my own hand, what does the timing matter?

9

r. Claude Horner tugged on his pearl-gray tie until
he got the knot just right. He shrugged his shoulders to settle the coat of his black suit a bit. Sometimes, when he was in the office, he covered his dress shirt and tie with a white coat. At other times, he wore that white coat over a set of surgical scrubs. Around the house, his dress was quite informal. But today he and his wife Nelda were attending the funeral of his partner's wife. And although he doubted that Henry Taggart would even notice, Claude felt he had an image to uphold, so he wore his best dark suit.

He gave his tie a final tug and moved to his wife's bedroom. He was a morning person, she was an evening person, and after several unsuccessful attempts to mesh their schedules or change them, they'd decided they slept better in separate rooms. They were happy with the arrangement, and Claude frankly didn't care if others thought it odd.

"About ready?" he asked.

Nelda looked at him approvingly. "Claude, you look quite handsome. Think this is okay?"

He thought his wife's navy-blue dress, accented with pearls and white cameo earrings, struck just the right note—fashionable yet subdued. "It looks fine."

"I guess having Nancy's service on Saturday was the best option," she said.

"I imagine this let some of Henry's colleagues attend." Claude hesitated. "Nelda, we need to talk about something before we leave. Let's sit down." He led her to the settee that was in the corner of her bedroom.

Nelda settled herself but frowned as she did so. "What's this about?"

"Let me explain what's gone on before you say anything more. And I definitely don't want you making a scene or storming out halfway through what I have to say."

She nodded, and—consciously or without thinking about it—began to slowly knead the lace handkerchief she pulled from her pocket.

"Throughout our marriage, I've always tried to share everything with you. I guess it's time to let you in on this."

She moved a bit further away from him. "You're scaring me, Claude. This sounds like you're about to confess something horrid. Are you having an affair? A midlife crisis?"

"No affair. Maybe sort of a midlife crisis, but not one that a new red sports car will solve."

"Well, tell me what's going on."

"Last night I went back to our building, wanting to check something in Henry's office. He was there, sitting at his desk, going over some papers. I couldn't see everything, because he shoved the work into his desk drawer as soon as he saw me. But I saw enough."

Nelda looked at her husband. "And I guess you're going to tell me what this means and why it's important."

Claude inched closer to her. "It's not just important. It may be the answer to all my problems."

He'd been married to Nelda for years. They'd been through ups and downs over the course of their marriage, and Claude didn't think she'd shy away from what he was about to share with her. But the only way to find out was to tell her.

Caden looked at his image in the motel room mirror. Beth had insisted she could go to Freeman alone to bring back clothes for the funeral, but he hadn't been about to let her. He guessed he didn't want to be left alone with his father and Jean. She seemed to have things well in hand, so he might as well be gone for a few hours.

At home, he'd pulled his dark brown suit out of the closet to wear for the service, but Beth gently vetoed that in favor of his dark gray one, with a white shirt and conservative tie. When Caden looked at himself, he had to agree that Beth's decision was the right one.

He looked at his watch. The limo provided by the funeral director would be arriving at Henry's home in another half hour. At least Jean had the decency not to ride with the family to the service.

Beth emerged from the bathroom. "About ready?"

Was Caden ready? How do you get ready for your mother's funeral? "I guess." He took his keys off the table and dropped them in his pocket. "It should take about ten minutes to get to Dad's house."

"Don't worry. We have plenty of time."

"Should we have moved from this motel to Dad's house?" Caden asked. "I just thought—"

"A lot of people might have done that, but I think you read your father correctly. I think Henry prefers to be alone." She checked the contents of her purse, nodded, and took her husband's arm. "Of course, that works out well for you. It's fairly obvious that you don't want to be there with Jean around."

"It's hard for me to accept the role she's taking right now."

"I realize that," Beth said. "But Henry needs all the support he can get—from you and from Jean. Try to put your differences with her aside for the moment. This will be tough enough for him to get through without your adding to the difficulty."

"I'll try."

Caden opened the door of their SUV and Beth climbed in. He then walked to the other side and slid under the wheel. She waved to Henry, who was standing on the front porch of his house.

Beth fastened her seat belt. "The funeral was just yesterday, and you already want to go back to Freeman? Are you sure you don't want to stay longer?"

Caden buckled in and started the car. "No, Dad doesn't need me here, and he probably wants me to go as badly as I want to head home."

"I can't believe that."

"I know my father, and I imagine he'd like to be alone. Besides, if he needs someone to talk with, there's always Jean."

Beth heard the emotion in her husband's voice but decided now wasn't the time to argue with him. She needed to talk with Caden about his resentment of Jean, but not so soon after Nancy's death. She'd steer around the subject for now. "I'm glad my folks came up for the funeral."

Caden didn't take his eyes off the road. "Yeah, I guess. Of course, they didn't stay very long."

"Would you rather they stayed longer? Both you and your father seemed to want them gone."

He thought that over. "No, I appreciate the gesture, and there wasn't anything they could have added." Caden glanced over at his wife. "Look, I'm still processing some stuff. And traffic is pretty heavy here. Why don't we talk about this later? Okay?"

After they'd cleared the Dallas city limits and were on the highway back to Freeman, Beth asked her husband, "When did your father think he would have his endoscopic ultrasound and biopsy?"

"He hasn't set a date yet," Caden said. "He called the oncologist to explain why he had to cancel the biopsy, but so far as I know he hasn't rescheduled it."

"I guess he'll let us know."

Caden shook his head. "I don't know if he's going through with it now."

"Because of your mother's death?"

"We talked about it. He and I both know that if this is really carcinoma of the pancreas the odds of survival for even a year are small. I tried to tell him those odds aren't zero, though, and he should move ahead." He passed a slower-moving panel van, then steered back into his own lane. "But I don't know what his plans are. One thing I've learned over the years. You don't tell my father what to do."

And he's passed that stubbornness down to his son. Beth waited a beat before saying, "I'm glad he has Jean to help him through this."

A light mist began to fall, and Caden turned the windshield wipers to an intermittent setting. Then, when he turned to reply, Beth was surprised at the expression on his face—she wasn't sure if it was anger or sorrow. Perhaps it represented a mixture. "I realize I resent what she's doing, and I can't get past it. I've sort of pigeonholed Jean as the person who took care of Dad at his office, but she was never a part of our private lives."

"And now she is," Beth said.

"And now she is," Caden repeated. "I suppose that's why I was so shocked when she opened the door for us at my father's house."

"And why you think she had something to do with your mother's death?"

Caden nodded, tight-lipped, and kept his eyes on the road.

They were almost to the Freeman city limits, and Caden was driving by habit and muscle memory. He wasn't really thinking about where he was going. Instead, his mind wandered over the transition from the death of his mother back to what he considered his "usual" life, which was by no means usual. He glanced to his right and saw Beth was dozing, her head against the window.

A vehicle approached Caden's Outback, and he instinctively moved a bit to his right in case they were going to pass. As it drew closer, he saw that it was a black Ford pickup truck. He remembered the teenagers who'd passed him on this stretch of road recently, and idly wondered if this was them. There were probably more pickups in this part of north Texas than there were sedans or SUVs, and it seemed most were black, so it was unlikely this was the same one.

Caden realized there was something not right about the way this one was behaving. As the truck came abreast of the Outback, it began to edge across the center line, crowding Caden's vehicle toward the shoulder.

Only there wasn't really a shoulder here. Instead, at this point a damaged metal guardrail ran along the right side of the narrow strip of concrete that marked the edge of the two-lane highway. The strips of metal were supposed to protect vehicles from dropping off the side and into the ditch that bordered the farm field to the right of the roadway. But a previous vehicle had flattened the guardrail, splintering the posts that held it, leaving nothing to keep Caden's vehicle from flipping down the embankment except his ability to steer clear of disaster.

There was no way Caden was about to get into a contest of strength with the pickup truck. He stomped down hard on the brake pedal and fought hard as he felt his SUV fishtail toward the ditch.

The pickup gave a final scrape to the left side of his vehicle before pulling away. Caden brought his SUV to a halt about the time Beth awoke with a start.

"What ... what's going on?" she asked.

"Are you okay?"

"I'm fine. But what happened?"

"Hang on a minute," Caden said. He left his SUV idling with the transmission in park. A quick check of his rearview mirror and a scan of the road ahead told him there were no other vehicles around. He opened the driver's side door and climbed out. The mirror on that side was sprung forward, but he was able to snap it back into place. The left front fender had a long crease from the near-collision, and the black paint that streaked it—probably from the pickup's fender or bumper—made a sharp contrast to the silver finish of the SUV. The crease was unsightly, but the fender wasn't pushed inward enough to interfere with steering, which was good. By and large, Caden felt he was lucky to get out of the near-collision with no more damage than this.

He climbed back under the wheel, still breathing a bit rapidly from the experience. "Somebody in a black Ford pickup tried to run us off the road."

"Are you okay?"

"I'm fine. Are you sure you're not hurt?"

"Just a little scared, I guess," she said. "Do you think it was an accident?"

"Well, to me there's no other explanation than the driver wanted to run us off the road," Caden said. "Alcohol? It's a little early in the day for the driver to be drunk. Did the rain leave the pavement slick, so the pickup skidded into us? It wasn't so wet I had trouble stopping." Caden touched Beth's arm. "No, I think this was deliberate."

"That brings up another part of the question," Beth said. "Who's behind this?"

"I don't know, but I think I'm going to start looking behind me more." Caden pulled out his cell phone, made certain he had reception, then dialed 9-1-1.

"Taggart's engaged a lawyer. Apparently, he's no longer content to stay out of the way and let us do what we came for."

"*Is he digging into your credentials? Wanting to see what you've found? Getting in the way?*"

"*He's curious, but he hasn't done anything that will interfere with what we're doing.*"

"*You don't think it's time to go to Plan B, do you?*"

"*Not yet, but if he keeps fighting back we may have to consider that.*"

"*Meanwhile?*"

"*Just a few more days and we'll disappear. He may be curious for a while, but soon he'll forget it. And the whistle-blower threat will go away.*"

"*If not?*"

"*Then we go to Plan B. We lay the blame on him and everyone will mourn him for a bit. We shut things down here and move on to another center. Either way, we're safe.*"

Henry's friends and acquaintances all told him to take a few days off—go somewhere, take his mind off recent events. His answer was to tell Jean to go by the office this weekend and make certain he had patients to see on Monday. If their appointment had been cancelled, call them—even though it was Sunday—and get them in. He wanted to stay busy.

His first patient was a case where a second opinion was required before the third-party payer would pre-authorize the surgery. The material the patient brought with her didn't fully support the need for surgery, but a phone call by Henry to the other doctor elicited some points not well documented in the records.

After he hung up, Henry thought a minute about something the other doctor said to him. "Sometimes it's good to get a fresh pair of eyes on the subject." Maybe he should take that advice in his own case. Perhaps he should … Henry shook his head. He wanted to think about that some more.

He went back to the exam room and tapped on the door before entering, carrying the chart he'd taken with him when he made his phone call. "Mrs. Williams, I needed some more information, and your surgeon is sending a couple of supplemental statements about your treatment and what he's observed. With those, I think I'll have no problem documenting my agreement with his decision to operate."

The woman frowned. "So, you really think he's doing the right thing?"

"Yes, I do," he said. "It's just that sometimes you need a second set of eyes on the problem in order to be certain."

As the patient left, Henry stopped Jean and said, "We'll be getting a fax from her surgeon. Put that, along with her chart and paperwork, on my desk."

"Very good, doctor." Then, in a much softer voice, Jean said, "Henry, how are you doing?"

"Not bad," Henry said. Then he thought of the option that had been percolating in the back of his mind for the past fifteen minutes. "Not bad at all."

He turned away, and Jean said, "Your next patient hasn't shown up, so you have a little free time."

"Good. I have something I need to do, and I don't want to put it off any longer."

In his office, with the door closed, Henry called several colleagues. He framed his questions as though his search was being made on behalf of a patient. After half a dozen calls, he checked out the website of the winner of his informal survey and decided that Dr. Bradley Ross was the person he wanted to see for a second opinion. He hadn't asked his son, even though Caden had trained at UT Southwestern and knew a lot of specialists in Dallas. Henry wanted this to be his decision and his alone. After all, it was his life that was at stake.

Gershwin was an oncologist, a specialist in cancer. Henry decided his second opinion would come from a practitioner of a different specialty. A well-trained gastroenterologist should be competent to establish the diagnosis of pancreatic cancer if it were present. As for treatment … Well, one step at a time.

Caden entered his office a bit later than usual on Monday and found the two DEA agents waiting for him. They were sitting in the patient chairs on the opposite side of his desk, so at least they hadn't taken over his office. He eased down into his swivel chair, leaned back, and said, "Well, gentlemen. Where do we stand?"

"We have some questions for you," Agent Neilson said.

Caden shook his head but didn't say anything.

"Perhaps you didn't hear us," Agent Harwell said.

"I heard perfectly, but I don't plan to say anything else to you unless it's in the presence of my attorney."

"Look," Neilson said. "We don't think you're at fault here. We just want some more information, so we can wrap this up."

Caden acted as though he hadn't heard a word the agent said. He pulled his patient list for the day toward him. "I'll contact my lawyer and see if we can set up a meeting at his office. If he has an opening late today, I can be there at four this afternoon. How shall I contact you?"

Harwell's face turned red. "We're the federal agents here, and we expect your cooperation. How would you like it if we marched you out of here in handcuffs?"

"I'd call my attorney, who'd have me out in a matter of hours. Then he'd file suit for false arrest and a few other things I'm certain he'll think of. Of course, he'd include your bosses in any such suit. And you could kiss any further cooperation on my part good-bye." He looked at Neilson, whom he'd pegged as the point man in this investigation. "I'll try to make this as painless as possible. Give me a cell phone number where I can contact you, and as soon as I talk with my attorney we'll set this up."

Harwell opened his mouth, but Neilson stopped him with an upraised hand. He reeled off ten numerals, which Caden entered into his cell phone. "I'd appreciate it if you'd try to set this up for later today."

Caden nodded. "I'll call you as soon as I know something."

Both agents rose and were about to leave when Neilson turned back from the partially opened door. "The other day you were anxious to cooperate. Now your attitude has changed. What happened?"

"I decided that I should stop worrying about your investigation and start being concerned with what was best with me." He smiled. "I highly recommend it."

10

Beth remembered an errand she had to run and decided to call Caden to see if he would like to meet her and eat somewhere after he got off work. The receptionist told her that her husband had left early for a meeting. No, she didn't know where the meeting was, or with whom, or how long it would last. Did she want to leave a message?

"No, that's okay."

"Wait a second. Here's Dr. Taggart's nurse. Let me see if he told her more about where he was going."

"Wait—." But it was too late. Beth heard the murmur of two voices, then a new one came on the line.

"This is Rose, Mrs. Taggart. All I know is that Dr. Taggart said he had an important meeting at his lawyer's office, so he absolutely had to leave by 3:30. Of course, he got away late—probably about 3:45. Did you want me to tell him something if he comes back here before we leave?"

"No, that's fine."

Beth could almost hear the concern in Rose's voice. "I was hoping this was the agency calling. I'd mentioned this to Dr. Taggart, but with all that's been going on he apparently forgot. We put out the information today, so I suppose it's unrealistic to expect someone to be applying for the position already."

"Applying? Position? What's that about?"

"Didn't your husband mention anything to you about this? I told him over a month ago. My husband is being transferred to Tulsa, so I'm leaving this position in just a few days." She sighed. "I reminded the doctor about it, but he seemed preoccupied."

I'm a trained and credentialed nurse. I've only worked in a hospital, but I'm intelligent enough to learn the duties of an office nurse. And I do so want to get out of the house.

"Rose, who's in charge of hiring your replacement?"

"I guess Dr. Taggart is."

"Well, don't fill the position until I have a chance to talk with him," Beth said.

"If Dr. Taggart comes by here after the meeting, shall I tell him you called?"

"No, don't say a word until I can talk with him. I think I have an idea about who your replacement will be."

Henry imagined that getting his records from Dr. Gershwin's office would be difficult—talking with the staff, explaining why he wanted copies of the material, even arguing if necessary. He was wrong. A phone call gave him the information he needed. If he submitted the required paperwork, copies of the records and X-rays would be available for him to pick up the next day. The nurse told him they usually sent them to the other doctor, but since Henry was a physician, they'd bend the rules a bit.

The next hurdle to clear was getting an appointment with the doctor he'd chosen for a second opinion. He dialed the number for Dr. Ross's office, expecting to work his way through a maze of recorded voices and options. Instead, he found the call was answered by a real, live person. "I need an appointment to see Dr. Ross," he said.

"Were you referred by your doctor?"

"I'm a physician—Dr. Henry Taggart. I've seen Dr. Gershwin at the medical center, but I want a second opinion. I'd like that to come from Dr. Ross."

The receptionist said, "One moment. Let me see what's available. I presume you want this quickly."

"Please." Now that he was ready to take the leap, Henry wanted an appointment immediately, but he knew that wasn't possible. After he assured the woman at the computer that he could get his doctor's notes and copies of the X-rays and bring them with him, they settled on a time on Thursday, a little more than two days away.

All that followed was a confirmation of his insurance coverage and a request that Henry go to their website and complete the new patient information. He hung up, made a note to get those papers filled out tonight, and settled down to do the hardest thing for him—as a surgeon and as a patient. Wait.

Caden didn't like to keep people waiting. He tried to stay on time with his appointments, although it didn't always work that way. But when someone took more than the allotted time, he asked his staff to advise the patients waiting about the delay (and, when it was possible to do so, the reason). That's just the way he was.

That was probably the reason he felt a bit ill at ease sitting next to Mel Sewell in the man's inner office while the two DEA agents cooled their heels in the lawyer's waiting room.

"Relax," Sewell said. "My main duty here is to protect your rights, and if it involves keeping those guys waiting while we confer, so be it."

Doctor and lawyer were seated next to each other at the table in one corner of Sewell's office. Two vacant chairs across the table from them awaited the men in the waiting room, but only after the attorney finished talking with Caden.

"Now, you've told me pretty much how it went down and where we are," Mel said. "Let me confirm though. They didn't have a warrant? They didn't show anything saying they had authority to investigate?"

Caden shook his head.

Mel gestured with his reading glasses. "Then they were fishing. They had a few instances where your DEA number was used in false prescriptions, but nothing to indicate you had anything to do other than being an innocent victim. They wanted to look around your office setup, and you let them use you."

Caden felt a blush creeping up his cheeks. "When these two guys showed up in my office, flashed their badges, and hinted about the bad things that were going on that might involve me, I was anxious to cooperate. Honestly, I was scared not to. But it's been a one-way street since then."

Sewell gave him a look that invited more information.

"They're keeping me in the dark about whether I've done anything wrong. It was almost as though they were holding it over my head. So, I finally decided that it was in my best interest to get legal counsel instead of just meekly going along with everything they want."

"And that was a wise move, although it would have been better if you'd done it as soon as they walked in the door," Mel said. "Before we call them in, let me tell you what I've found out with a few phone calls." He flipped through the pages on the legal pad in front of him. "There are indeed agents named Darren Neilson and Jerry Harwell based out of the Seattle office. Their pictures match the description you gave me. They were transferred there from DC and New York respectively. Neilson has a history of being just a little suspect, but nothing was ever proven. Harwell has one accusation in his personnel jacket of taking a payoff, but when the claim was investigated nothing was found."

"I never thought to check up on them," Caden said.

"Some of this information came through back channels," Mel replied. "The Seattle office of the DEA ordered them sent here because there seems to be a drug ring in Freeman. They were given this assignment because no one here knew them."

"That's what they told me."

Sewell turned a page on his legal pad. "Your office seemed to be where most of the illegal prescriptions originated. They didn't have enough to apply for a search warrant, so the agents blustered in and tried to frighten you into cooperating. And you did."

"So, what do I do now?"

"First, get them to admit that they've found nothing on you. Then offer them your continued assistance, in return for a free exchange of information."

They conferred for a few more minutes before Mel said, "Well, let's have them in and see what we can work out."

He went to his desk and called his secretary on the intercom. "Please show the two gentlemen in."

Mel met them at the door and escorted them to their chairs. When everyone was seated, he said, "Gentlemen, I'm sure you won't mind showing me your credentials." He waited until the two wallets with badges and ID cards were in front of him. Mel copied the information onto a fresh page of his yellow legal pad before shoving the badge cases back toward the men.

Neilson appeared frustrated by what had already gone on. "We don't appreciate the way—"

Mel raised his hand, palm outward, and waited until the room was quiet. "My client has been quite cooperative in allowing you two access to his practice's routine—especially in the absence of a warrant or court order. And he's willing to continue to be helpful, but it's a two-way street, starting now." He looked first at Neilson, then at Harwell. "So, who'd like to start the flow of information back in our direction?"

Beth was waiting for Caden to come through the door. He dropped his backpack and stepped into her arms for the hug and kiss they always exchanged when he came home. But when he turned loose, he sniffed and frowned.

"What's for supper? I have a lot to tell you."

"As do I," Beth answered. "And we can tell each other all about it over dinner—at RJ's."

Caden had unbuttoned the top button of his shirt and tugged his tie loose as he came in the door. Slowly, he re-did all that. "Fine. I don't mind taking you out to dinner, but what are we celebrating?"

"You'll see."

Fifteen minutes later, they sat in a back booth of their favorite restaurant. R.J. Terrell himself seated them, placing menus in front of them. "We don't see you folks much anymore," he said. "Must be sort of a special occasion."

Caden nodded, although Beth was certain from the look on his face that her husband had no idea what it was. "I think tonight I'd like one of RJ's specialties. How do you feel about splitting a Chateaubriand?"

She could see the wheels turning in Caden's head. The Chateaubriand was essentially a large steak, the choicest cut, cooked with a sauce that always made Caden's mouth water. There were potatoes and other vegetables on the side, but the meat was what he always talked about. Beth never tried it at home, but they both always enjoyed it at RJ's.

"Sounds great to me, but I still want to know what the occasion is."

"I talked with Rose this afternoon. Actually, I called to see if you wanted to join me for dinner out. Instead, I got some interesting information from her, information that gave me an idea."

"What? Oh, did she tell you about her husband's new job and the upcoming move? In all that's been going on, I sort of pushed that news to the back of my mind. She's going to start the process of getting some applicants."

Beth shook her head. "No, she isn't."

Caden frowned. "Didn't I tell her to do that?"

"And I told her to stop. When I found out about this, I decided it was a great opportunity for me to get back to work." She took a deep breath and plunged on. "I'm a trained, certified, credentialed nurse who's been sitting at home because you want to eventually start a family. Well, that process hasn't produced any results, and until it does, I'm ready to work."

He opened his mouth, but she went right ahead.

"Rose can train me. It shouldn't take long for me to pick up the routine. I'm sure the nurses for the other two doctors will help as well. And before you open your mouth, I've heard all the arguments about wives working with their husbands, but I don't see why we can't do it." She looked at her husband.

Before Caden could answer, the waitress was at their table, asking to take their drink orders.

"Two iced teas. And we're going to share a Chateaubriand, medium-well, with all the trimmings."

"Very good," the waitress said. "Sounds like this is some sort of a special evening."

Beth nodded. "I think it will be before we're through."

Caden wiped his lips with the napkin and dropped it on the table. He'd eaten a bit more than his half of the steak, using a roll to mop up the last part of the sauce on his plate. Over dinner, Beth had managed to overcome each objection he raised. Finally, Caden gave in.

"You know, I guess this solution has an advantage we haven't covered. It gives your mother one less thing to complain about," he said.

"We'll work on the rest of what you call her trifecta of complaints later, but until then I'm glad to get back into nursing."

When the waitress came to clear the dishes, both Beth and Caden passed on dessert but asked for coffee. They sat, each lost in their own thoughts, until they were served.

Caden stirred sweetener into his coffee. "I have some news of my own I want to share with you." Seeing her upraised brows, he continued. "I met with the two DEA agents and my attorney this afternoon."

"Tell me about it."

He looked around, but things were quiet at RJ's that Monday evening. There was no one within earshot of the booth they occupied. "Mel Sewell told me I shouldn't have rolled over and complied so easily with the requests of those men. Once he set some ground rules, they told me a bit more about their investigation. To begin with, they admitted they've found no evidence that I'm involved in what amounts to a drug ring centered here in Freeman."

"I never thought you were."

"You can be as pure as the driven snow, as the saying goes, but there's still the possibility you can get caught up in the net. Once we established my innocence, the agents told me that thus far they've found my name and DEA number aren't being used on written prescriptions for controlled substances. They're being used via the EPCS."

"The what?" Beth asked.

"This is something you've never really been involved with because you worked on a hospital ward. Doctors used to have to jump through a number of hoops to prescribe narcotics. They could call in an emergency prescription but had to follow it up with a written one within a day or two. Here in Texas, the EPCS system was adopted in 2010."

"I still don't know what EPCS is."

"Electronic prescription for controlled substances. Not all doctors' offices use it, but it's nice for those prescribing narcotics frequently. We used to have to follow up an emergency phone prescription with a written one. That's all changed."

"Tell me about the EPCS," Beth said. "How does it work?"

"A nurse or physician, under the authority of a qualified prescriber, can use this electronic system to send a controlled substance prescription to a pharmacy. There are things they have to do, some of which I don't try to understand, because not all pharmacies are set up to receive these scripts. But we've been using this system in the office since right after it started up."

"For just you?"

"No, for all three of the doctors. Our DEA number isn't particularly secret, and each of our nurses is authorized to use the electronic system for all our prescriptions, not just narcotics. It saves a lot of writing for the doctors."

Beth took a sip of her coffee, then shoved it aside. "So, have the agents identified who's doing this?"

"Not yet. Prescriptions using each doctor's DEA number have showed up at a number of pharmacies. This is a well-organized ring, and although the agents want to learn who the person or people involved are, they also hope to uncover the person who's behind it."

"Will they still be around your office?"

The waitress came by with a coffeepot. Caden checked with Beth, then declined and asked for the check.

"Harwell says he's about finished at my office, but they'll both be in town for a bit longer." Caden frowned.

"I'm wondering if your showing up to start work there is going to make some waves."

"I think the nurses will accept me."

Caden shook his head. "As a nurse, I'm sure they will. But what if the person who's been inputting the fake scripts thinks you're there to spy on them?"

11

"Have you heard anything more about our near-crash on Saturday?" Beth said as she emerged from their bathroom on Tuesday morning.

"My 9-1-1 call went to the sheriff, since the accident happened outside the city limits," Caden said. He pulled on his socks and reached for his shoes. "I forgot to tell you they called me yesterday afternoon. The driver of that pickup hit someone else later that morning, and they arrested him. He was a drunk teenager."

"Drunk at that time of the morning?"

"The party he attended started on Friday night and was just breaking up when he hit us on Saturday," Caden said. "I guess our accident didn't have anything to do with this DEA investigation."

"I'd still be careful," Beth said. "What do the nurses at your office wear?"

"Uh, I haven't paid much attention."

"I assume it's scrub suits of some sort, covered by a jacket. Do the doctors insist on a certain color? Is there a style I need to match?" Beth laughed. "I doubt they wear white dresses and nurse's caps like you see in some of the old movies."

Caden shook his head. "Why don't you wear what you did at your last job? If there's a problem, you can deal with it later."

Beth was pleased that her clothes from her prior work as a ward nurse still fit. She packed a lunch, in case there was no time to go out and eat. Was there anything else she needed to take? If so, she'd deal with it later.

When she was ready to leave, Caden said, "Want to ride with me?"

"And what do we do if you have an emergency case, or have to go by the hospital to see a consult? No, I'm a big girl. We'll take two cars."

Beth arrived at eight o'clock and found a parking place with ease. She figured that her scrubs should have provided a clue, but the receptionist probably had no idea who she was or why she was there. She could just as easily have entered the suite to ask directions to some other office.

"May I help you?"

"I'm Beth, the new nurse. I don't know if Dr. Taggart told Rose to expect me, but…"

The young blonde rose and extended her hand. "I'm Donna. Welcome." She bent over and flipped a switch before she spoke. "Rose, come to the front, please."

In a moment, an older brunette, her glasses hanging by a chain around her neck, came through a door that apparently led to the treatment area. Beth guessed that the woman was in her mid-50s. She was a bit stout, although not obese. In addition to a watch on her left wrist, the woman wore a wedding ring on her left hand. She extended the right, and said, "Welcome. Dr. Taggart didn't call to give me a heads-up, but I spoke with his wife yesterday afternoon and she sort of led me to believe they had someone in mind for the position."

Obviously neither of the women had recognized Beth's voice from the phone call. She had always left off her rings and other jewelry when she worked on a hospital ward, and she'd done that today when she donned what she considered her "nursing uniform." Further, Beth hadn't used her name when introducing herself to the receptionist.

Would it be best to keep her identity as "the doctor's wife" secret? No, there was no reason to start her employment with a lie. Besides, what if she wanted to go into his office and close the door? Neither she nor Caden needed to start that kind of rumor. Beth decided to go with the axiom she'd heard before: Tell the truth. That way, you don't have to remember what you said.

"Actually, Rose, I'm here to learn the ropes so I can be your replacement." She extended her hand. "I'm Elizabeth Taggart, but everyone calls me Beth."

Caden walked into the front hall of his home and paused to sniff. He'd become used to entering and smelling the odors of that night's dinner. But there was none of that. He hadn't fully realized until then that he'd come to rely on his evening meal being ready shortly after he arrived home.

He thought about it and realized the many things that Beth did to keep their house running—little things he'd taken for granted since their marriage. Grocery shopping. Laundry. Cooking. Cleaning. How would she have time to do all that now that she was working? Of course, he'd help, but would that be enough? He began to have second thoughts about her working as his office nurse.

The house was quiet, and as he moved through it Caden realized that Beth wasn't home yet. Should he call her cell phone? No, if she needed him, she'd let him know. Beth, along with the rest of the staff, was still at the office when he left to go to the hospital. His visit there, a couple of consultations and a bit of conversation with some of his colleagues, had taken a while. But shouldn't Beth be home by now? He'd never given any thought to the things that had to be done by his nurse before she left for the day.

He heard the garage door open, followed by the noise of her Outback pulling in. A moment later, Beth entered through the kitchen. She dropped the bag of groceries she carried and gave him a hug. "Been home long?"

"Not really." Caden had a dozen questions but figured Beth would probably tell him all he wanted to know as she unloaded the food.

"I think I can throw something together if you're able to wait a bit," she said over her shoulder.

"Sure. Is there anything I can do to help?"

"Nope. This won't take long." Beth pointed to a chair at the kitchen table. "Have a seat."

One question in Caden's mind had already been answered. While he had worried about Beth working at the office, she apparently enjoyed it. He pulled out a kitchen chair and listened as she recounted the events of the day from her perspective.

"I think I'll catch on easily to the routine of working in a doctor's office," she said, as she bustled around the kitchen. "And Rose is a good teacher."

"Have you met everyone on staff yet?"

Beth pulled a package of chicken breasts from the freezer and put it into the microwave to defrost. "I worked mainly with your nurse, Rose. I also met Mona, Dr. Russell's nurse, and Gary, the nurse for Dr. Sparling, but I didn't really have much interaction with them."

"Were they cordial?"

"Mona was. Gary seemed a bit ... I don't know. He was a little distant."

"That's just Gary's personality, I think," Caden said. "He came here looking for a job at about the time Jim Sparling was getting ready to open his practice. I presume Jim checked his background, and he's worked out fine."

The microwave beeped. She checked the meat, hit some buttons again, and turned back to Caden. "I'd already met Donna, one of the two receptionists. I think Mona, the other one, was off today. So I guess that's everybody."

"Sounds like you had a full day," Caden said. "Did you have any trouble with charts?"

"No. Rose showed me how to pull them up. You have a few of the old ones in paper form, but not many."

Caden nodded. "Did Rose show you how to use the electronic prescription function?"

"She touched on the basics—the usual meds, refills, things like that."

"What about narcotics?"

Beth shook her head. "She said you rarely prescribe controlled substances, so we didn't get into that today."

"Did she show you where to find my DEA number?" Caden asked.

"We went to the file room and she showed me the computer all the nurses use to write and send prescriptions. I mainly learned about the regular meds, but I noticed that the DEA numbers for all three doctors are posted on the wall right next to a listing of the most popular pharmacies that accept electronic prescriptions."

He nodded but said nothing. Surely the DEA agents saw this too. It was obvious that anyone with access to the office suite could send electronic prescriptions and make it look like they were authorized by any of the physicians. He probably should change this. Of course, that might be locking the barn door after the horse was long gone. He'd ask Neilson about it.

The other question in his mind was one he planned to investigate without mentioning it to the DEA agents. If this leak in the security of their system was so evident, why had Harwell spent so much time in the office?

Wednesday was busy but enjoyable for Beth. Dr. Sparling had a surgical case canceled for that morning, but there was room in the suite for both him and Dr. Taggart to see patients. Dr. Russell had also been there for a few minutes that morning, but after receiving an urgent call from the hospital she'd left.

"What's up with that patient of Dr. Russell's," Beth said to Mona.

"I think there was a patient in the emergency room who had a bleeding aortic aneurysm," the other nurse replied. "That was what I gathered as she took out of here."

Beth had seen the other side of this scenario—the surgeon rushing in to operate on an emergency case, but never gave much consideration to the juggling of schedules that went on back at the doctor's office. She had to admire Donna and Mona, both of whom had gone through this often enough that they seemed comfortable. She wondered if she'd ever achieve that level of ease when called upon.

"Phone call for Dr. Taggart," Donna said. "It's Dr. Russell, and I think it's urgent."

Beth nodded and headed down the hall, where she met Caden coming out of his office. "Call from Dr. Russell."

"Usually this is about a patient. Let's see what she wants." He ducked back into his office and punched the lighted button for the back line while Beth waited in the hall.

A moment later, Caden hurried into the corridor. "Beth, get Rose and Donna to help you with rescheduling my morning patients. I'll be in surgery for the next several hours." Before she could comment, he pushed open the back door and left.

Beth thought about what she'd been considering just moments before. *Well, I guess it's time to find out how good a juggler I am.*

Caden scrubbed in as soon as he arrived at the OR, and it didn't take him long to see that the patient's aortic aneurysm—the balloon-like dilation of the major blood vessel running from the heart to his pelvis—was leaking blood faster than Ann's efforts to control it.

Ann kept her eyes on the operative field when Caden took his place across the table from her. "Thanks for coming. I need to get the graft in place, but I'm not getting anywhere because of the bleeding."

"How do you want me to help?"

"Start with some more retraction."

Caden repositioned the instruments that allowed him to expose the area where Ann was working. "Better?"

"Not much." Ann looked up at the scrub nurse. "I need more suction. And get someone to adjust the light. Maybe bring in another spot. I can't see anything in this hole."

In situations like this, the surgeon's full attention was focused on the task at hand. Caden was surprised when he looked at the clock on the OR wall and saw he'd been a part of this procedure for more than an hour. Ann had finally given up on the preferred maneuver of inserting a graft to reroute blood to vital organs before resecting the section of aorta that was bleeding. Instead, she cross-clamped the large vessel to replace it with the graft before there was permanent damage. If she couldn't restore circulation quickly, the patient would lose his legs, perhaps his kidneys, maybe even his life.

Ann worked fast and Caden tried to match her speed, all the while keeping a silent count of how long the perfusion had been compromised. Just as Ann and Caden were releasing the clamps that would allow blood to begin flowing again to these areas, the anesthesiologist shook his head. "He's flat-lined. No pulse. No pressure. I couldn't pump in blood as fast as he was hemorrhaging. I've tried adding plasma expanders and colloids, but it was a losing battle." He paused. "Sorry. He's gone."

Before he lost his first patient during surgery, Caden somehow imagined there would be silence in the operating room after a patient died on the table. But he discovered that wasn't the case, just as it wasn't in this instance. The ambient sounds changed a bit, but the room was far from silent.

He could hear the muted ringing of a phone at the OR secretary's desk ninety feet away. Voices, although hushed, still echoed from the tiled walls in the hallway. And in the operating room where he stood, the normal sounds of surgery were replaced by the soft voices of two nurses who were preparing the body of the patient for transport to the morgue.

Caden leaned back against the OR wall, trying to work the kinks out of his back and relieve the muscle spasms brought on by working in a cramped position for so long. With his mask dangling around his neck, he flipped off his gloves and shucked out of his blood-soaked gown. He tossed them in the bin and looked up at the ceiling. As far as Caden knew, Ann had done everything she could, but he knew she'd be depressed because she'd been unable to save the man. He knew he would be.

Ann had sounded so confident on the phone, sort of like, "I'll take care of this, but I sure could use your help." Now she stood silently at the writing shelf that extended from the OR wall and scribbled notes for the patient's chart. Later there'd be a full operative note to dictate, all the paperwork that went with an operation, even when the result was the death of the patient.

Although she was writing, Caden knew Ann's mind was on what was coming next. She was getting ready to face the man's family to tell them, "I did everything I could, but he didn't survive. I'm sorry." Caden knew it, because he'd been in her position before. And no matter how many times a doctor faced that situation, it never got easier.

Caden was certain what the answer would be, but he asked anyway. "Would you like me to go with you to talk with the family?"

Ann was shaking her head before he finished his offer. "Thanks, but they won't know you. Actually, they don't know me either. There was no family with the man when I saw him in the ER." She started to turn away, then looked back at him. "But I'd appreciate it if you'd wait around for me. I think it might help to talk about this with someone who understands."

"Of course," Caden said. He made sure the OR nurses didn't need anything from him, then went to the surgeons' dressing room to change out of his bloody scrubs into his street clothes. It probably wouldn't hurt to shower first either.

After Caden had cleaned up and changed clothes, he looked in the surgeon's lounge for Ann, but she was nowhere to be seen. He sat on the couch, fidgeting and checking his watch several times. What was taking her so long?

Caden knew why she didn't want him with her when she talked with the family of the patient who had just died. As she'd pointed out, they didn't know him. And undoubtedly Ann was as experienced as he at breaking news of a loved one's death to the family. But he also understood her request that he stick around. Caden knew after losing a patient it helped to talk through the experience with someone who understood.

After waiting for fifteen more minutes, Caden began to have second thoughts about his promise to Ann. They probably needed him back at the office. Should he call Beth? He could tell her he was still at the hospital but out of surgery. There might even be a question or two he could answer over the phone.

Caden had his cell phone out when the door of the lounge opened, and Ann Russell entered. She, too, had changed out of her scrubs, and when she sat down beside him, Caden could smell the soap and shampoo she'd just used in her shower.

He put his phone back in his pocket and decided to let Ann speak first. They sat in silence for a moment, and when she finally spoke, she surprised him. He thought she'd want to talk about the medical aspects of the operation. What could she have done differently? Was there something she'd missed that could have altered the outcome?

Instead, she sighed, then said quietly, "There was no one for me to talk with."

Caden furrowed his brow. "I don't understand."

"The patient presented to the emergency room with severe belly pain. I found out that he took a bus to the hospital because there was no one to bring him. When I went out to talk with the family, there was nobody in the waiting area. When he signed into the ER, he listed a chaplain at a rescue mission as his emergency contact, so I called there. No one knew anything about him other than his name."

"No family, no friends?" Caden asked.

"No one. That really upset me."

"What did?"

"He didn't have any friends, anyone who cared if he lived or died. And when you think about it, neither do I."

Caden's response was made without conscious thought. "Of course, you do."

"Think about it. I have a few professional acquaintances," she said. "When you ask me to name my friends I think of you, but I wonder about that. I've never been in your home. I know your wife's name is Beth, but until she started working at the office the other day, I'd met her maybe twice. I wonder if I really have any friends. Does anyone care if I live or die?"

"What about your parents?"

"Divorced." Ann sighed. "Although they'd never say it, I think they thought I was a precipitating factor, so they decided to drop me when their marriage came apart. I haven't talked with either of them for a couple of months, and when I did, I was the one who called them."

Caden started to protest, but Ann wasn't finished.

"You're the only one who cares about me." She moved even closer to him. "And I don't want to die alone like that man."

"Ann, you're not—"

Before he finished his sentence, Ann put one arm around his neck, pulled him toward her, and kissed him.

12

Caden knew he was running behind when he finally left the hospital, and spent the rest of the afternoon at the office catching up. But when he had a moment to stop and think, guilt swept over him about Ann's kiss. She'd immediately apologized, saying her emotions got the best of her. Caden had told her to forget it. But he couldn't take his own advice. He couldn't forget, couldn't stop wondering about Ann's motivation and feelings for him. Did he return the kiss? He didn't think so, but was the act a betrayal of Beth?

He'd known Ann since their days together in residency. There was no question she was beautiful—an attractive blonde who was unattached, a perfect catch for someone. She'd been cool with most men, rebuffing approaches from unmarried and married men alike, yet her relationship with Caden had always been that of friend and colleague. She'd never shown any evidence of wanting to take their connection beyond a professional one—until now.

Another factor, and one Caden couldn't fully figure out, was the relationship of agent Jerry Harwell and Ann. Caden had thought from the first time Harwell laid eyes on her that there was an attraction there—at least on the agent's part. But Ann had kept things cool. Had that changed?

At the end of the workday, before he left the office, Beth stopped Caden. "Would you mind if I didn't cook tonight? I've got a headache, and all I want to do is slip into comfortable clothes and sit in front of the TV watching mindless shows."

"Why don't I order a pizza? But before you get too engrossed in TV—or, more likely, fall asleep in front of the set—I need to talk with you a bit."

"About something here at the office?"

Caden shook his head. "Not exactly. But we can discuss this more at home."

It was almost time for Beth to get home, and Caden hoped he was ready. He had a large pizza warming in the oven. Although he'd always considered pizza to be finger food, to be eaten directly out of the box or—at least—off paper plates, he'd set the dining room table with real china, as well as knives and forks. Glasses of iced tea sat beside both plates. Too much? He hoped not.

Beth walked in the door, dropped her purse, kicked off her shoes, and started to collapse onto the sofa next to Caden. Then she lifted her nose and sniffed. "I do believe I smell pizza."

"Welcome to Chez Caden." He chuckled and kissed her quickly, then led her into the dining room.

"All this for pizza?" She looked at him askew.

He gestured her to a seat and pulled out the chair for her. "There's nothing too good for my working wife."

She giggled as he fetched the pizza and served it on the china plates.

Beth asked a blessing that Caden thought was a little too long for carry-out, but he bowed his head and waited patiently for her to finish, even though his stomach churned with hunger.

After each of them consumed their first piece, he said in a mock-British accent, "I suppose you're wondering why I've called this meeting tonight."

Beth smiled, which Caden took as a good sign. "Seriously, I have something I need to tell you."

She dropped her second piece of pizza on the plate and looked at him. "Did you hear from your father today?"

"No."

"Is there something new in the DEA investigation?"

"Not really."

Beth shook her head. "Then what is it? Something that has to do with the office? Is there a problem with my work?"

"No. You've caught on to the routine like I knew you would." Caden drank some of his iced tea, but his throat still felt dry. "Ann's patient was bleeding from an abdominal aneurysm. The hemorrhage was too fast for us, and he died on the table."

"That's terrible. Is that why you've seemed preoccupied all afternoon?"

"No. I mean, no doctor likes to lose a patient, but Ann and I did everything we could. That wasn't what I was thinking about this afternoon."

"Then what?"

"Ann asked me to wait around to talk a bit after she notified the family," Caden said. "But when she came back, she found that the patient didn't have one—at least, no one who seemed to care. Then she started talking about who might care if she lived or died."

"I can understand that reaction."

"Then I hope you can understand this." Caden took a deep breath. "She kissed me."

Beth was silent for a moment, staring at him. When she spoke, he could tell she was trying hard to keep her voice level and her tone non-accusatory. "Do you think she was just reacting to the situation and her emotions?"

"I wish I knew." He stopped and frowned. "Her relationship with me has been the exception, but in general she's avoided attempts from other men to get close to her."

"What are you thinking? I can almost see the wheels turning in your head. Care to share?"

Caden looked into his wife's eyes. "First of all, I'm glad you don't think I made a play for Ann—at least, I don't think you do. And what she did could be blamed on the situation and her emotions. But part of me thinks about what's going on with the DEA and false narcotics prescriptions, and I have to wonder if this signals an attempt to either divert my attention or recruit me as an ally."

"Are you going to mention it to the agents?"

"Maybe to Neilson," Caden said. "I don't think I want to talk with Harwell about it though."

When Caden passed Ann in the OR on Thursday morning, she nodded and said, "Hi," then went on her way as though nothing had transpired between the two of them. Maybe her reaction had really come from the tension of the surgery, the disappointment of losing a patient, and the let-down when she compared the absence of friends and family in the life of the man who'd just died with her own life. Caden walked on eggs around her and watched for further signs.

At noon, he went into his office and closed the door. Neilson had promised that the investigation would be winding down soon, but when was "soon?" Mel Sewell had made Caden realize that he'd been cooperating with the men who showed up unannounced in his office without getting any information back. And even after they promised that would change, he'd seen no real evidence of it.

He picked up his phone to call Neilson, but quickly replaced the receiver. He'd use his cell phone. That way, there was no danger of someone in the office picking up their phone and accidentally overhearing his conversation. As he punched in the cell phone number Neilson had given him, Caden wondered if he was getting paranoid about the whole situation. Better safe than sorry. At least, that's what his father used to tell him. Most of the lessons of his life at home though came from his mother.

Neilson's answer to the call was a neutral, "Yes?"

"Agent, this is Dr. Taggart. Can you talk?"

"Not really."

"Is someone there with you?"

"Yes."

"Let me give you my cell number. Call me when you can talk freely." Caden reeled off the numbers, waited while Neilson repeated them back, and pushed the button to end the conversation. Now came the waiting.

Caden kept his cell phone in his pocket all afternoon, but Nielson never called. Had he decided not to get back in touch with him? Was the agent busy? Were the arrests that Neilson promised imminent? Caden wondered which of the nurses or office staff might be involved in the drug ring the DEA agents were investigating. He couldn't picture any of them as the perpetrator. Then again, he hadn't thought it possible that two men would show up at his office and turn his life upside down.

About the time Caden was ready to leave for the day, his cell phone buzzed. He looked at the display and saw that the identity of the caller was blocked. Should he answer? Yes. This was probably Neilson calling back. Caden stepped into his office and closed the door before he answered.

"Dr. Taggart?"

The voice on the other end of the call was distorted, and the words were difficult to make out because of an electronic frying sound. "Yes. Look, can I call you back? There seems to be a lot of static on this line."

"Can't. We need to meet somewhere safe. Can you come to this location right now?"

The site Neilson directed him to was probably a twenty-minute drive away, outside the city limits of Freeman in an isolated area. "I guess I can," Caden said. "But why—"

"You'll see." This was followed by a click.

Caden found Beth and told her he was going to meet Neilson. He didn't know when he'd make it home. If he was needed, call his cell phone.

"Do you want me to come with you?"

"He didn't specifically say to come alone, but I think that's what I'd better do," Caden said.

On Thursday afternoon, Henry made his way to the office of the gastroenterologist he had chosen. Dr. Bradley Ross was much younger than Dr. Gershwin, but along the way Henry had found that the man was already gaining a reputation as a top-notch practitioner in his specialty in the Dallas area. Unlike Gershwin, he didn't keep an office at the medical school, but was a clinical associate professor there, donating his time on a regular basis to teaching residents and fellows.

From the time Henry walked through the door of Ross's office, he was impressed. The waiting room was nicely appointed, but the way the staff behaved was what sold him. The receptionist was pleasant and helpful. The registration process was efficient. He handed over his records and a DVD that documented his radiology procedures. Although he had to fill out the usual forms, he didn't have to wait long before a middle-aged woman in a nurse's smock appeared at the doorway and called, "Dr. Taggart?" Although Henry didn't really want special treatment, he couldn't help but be pleased that the office staff at least recognized his profession and title.

After the standard weigh-in and recording of vital signs, he settled down in the exam room to wait. *Now we'll see how long I have to sit here.* The answer was "not long." Less than ten minutes later, Dr. Ross tapped on the door and entered.

The young man—at least, he looked young to Henry—smiled, introduced himself, and took a seat on the rolling stool next to the exam table. Ross was blond, with a ruddy complexion. A clean lab coat covered his pale blue dress shirt and patterned tie. Maybe it was because he dealt with GI issues, rather than cancer all day, but to Henry, Ross seemed pleasant compared to Gershwin.

"Dr. Taggart, I'm Brad Ross. How can I help you?"

"Would you like to see my records and tests before you get started?" Henry asked. "I brought them."

"I'd prefer to hear your story first." Ross leaned forward a bit. "Then we'll look at the tests together and decide where to go from there."

It took Henry about ten minutes to tell his story. Ross listened intently, occasionally jotting down a note but never interrupting. When Henry had finished, Ross asked a few questions, then was silent for a moment as he appeared to digest the information.

Finally, he rose from the stool and pulled a stethoscope from the pocket of his white coat. "Next I want to examine you. Why don't you slip off your shirt?"

The exam took another ten minutes and was thorough. Ross didn't say anything during the procedure, and Henry found it almost impossible to read his expression.

"After you're dressed, we'll look at the GI series," the gastroenterologist said. "That's what started you and your doctor on this trail."

In Ross's office, Henry handed over the DVD that showed his initial X-rays. The consultant popped the disc into the laptop computer on the desk and invited Henry to come around, so they could look at the radiographs together. Ross watched silently, often going back and forth to observe the passage of the contrast material through the intestinal tract. Finally, he turned to Henry and pointed to the area where the duodenum made its characteristic loop before the small intestine proper began. "So, the radiologist and your internist both thought the widening of this C-loop suggested a space-occupying lesion in the head of the pancreas."

"That's right," Henry said. "They felt it probably indicated early pancreatic carcinoma."

"Well, that's certainly possible, but further workup is necessary," Ross said. "Many times, that's a valid diagnostic clue, but it's not a slam dunk." He ejected the DVD and looked for the next one. "Let's check the ultrasound scan."

"I haven't had one yet. The consultant suggested a CT scan, and I have that here." Henry pushed forward another DVD.

Ross said, almost to himself, "I wonder why he did the CT next." As he put the disc in the laptop, he said, "We'll look at it because we have it, but as we both know, it will take a biopsy to definitively establish the diagnosis."

Henry nodded. *Well, he's not jumping to conclusions anyway.*

Ross was silent as he went through each of the views from the CT. After he'd finished, he went back and enlarged a couple of them. Then he pointed with the blunt end of his pen. "Here's a space-occupying lesion in the pancreas. It's not very large, but certainly large enough to widen the C-loop. It also showed up on the initial GI series. I suppose your consultant ordered the CT scan to confirm it."

"Do you agree that there's something there?"

Ross nodded. "It was pretty perceptive of your internist to follow up the abnormality on the GI series. I just hate to put a name to it until we actually have a biopsy and see the cells within the mass."

"So, what do you think?"

"The CT shows it's solid, so it's unlikely to be a pancreatic cyst. The next logical step is a needle biopsy. That's done with an endoscope you swallow—"

"I know how it's done," Henry interrupted. "But if it's pancreatic cancer, there's not a lot that treatment can offer. Aren't we just expending a lot of effort for nothing?"

"We aren't sure what the mass represents. We won't know until we look at some tissue," Ross said. "The studies raise the possibility of carcinoma of the pancreas, but even that's not a death sentence. There are things that we can do, but first comes the biopsy."

"I—"

Ross held up his hand. "I note from the papers you filled out that you're here for a second opinion. You're a doctor, but I'm going to simplify it anyway. You have a mass in the head of the pancreas that may represent a malignancy. I agree with Dr. Gershwin that an endoscopic ultrasound and needle biopsy are the next step. It appears to me that, like a lot of patients, you've been putting off moving forward, hoping all this would go away." He shook his head. "It won't."

"So, your opinion ..."

"Endoscopic ultrasound and needle biopsy, and the sooner the better. If they're positive, it's not a death sentence. But putting them off might be." Ross put his hand on Henry's chart but made no effort to open it. "Now you've had two doctors tell you what the next step should be. Whether you want the work performed by Dr. Gershwin at the medical center or by me is your decision. What do you want to do?"

"*He's got a lawyer involved now. He wants to know everything we've found out. This isn't going down the way we thought.*"

"*Do you have what you need to pull out and whitewash the whole thing?*"

"*Almost, but I think it would be easier to blame the whole thing on Taggart ... after he's dead.*"

"*So that means plan B.*"

"*It's already been activated.*"

Beth was the last one out the door of the office. She had her hand on the doorknob when she heard the phone ring. She had already checked out to the answering service, so she knew that after a couple of rings the call would go to them. If it was something Caden should respond to, the service would call his cell phone and give him the message.

She stood in the hall and listened for a moment. That was two rings ... then another ... and another. The call wasn't going to the answering service. Someone had dialed the unlisted, back line number. Beth reinserted her key, opened the door, and strode toward the front desk. This could just be a wrong number, but each of the doctors and nurses also had this number, so it might be important.

She lifted the receiver and punched the flashing button. "Dr. Taggart's office."

"This is ... er ... Dr. Neilson. Is Dr. Taggart there?"

"This is his wife. I know who you really are, Agent Neilson." Beth told him about the cell phone call Caden had received. "He left a little while ago."

"I didn't call him," Neilson said. "I've gone from meeting to meeting all day long, and just now got free where I could go somewhere private and call him. He's not answering his cell, so I decided to call him here."

"How did you get this unlisted number?"

"That's not important. But if he isn't there and he's not answering his cell, how am I supposed to get in touch with him?"

"Wait a minute. The call he got wasn't from you?"

"No. It wasn't from me."

A queasy feeling swept over Beth. Who had called Caden? And, where was he?

As Caden drove along the route laid out in the phone call, he saw city buildings give way to dwellings—apartments, then homes, then farm houses set far enough back from the road they were essentially isolated. During this time, traffic along the road he was driving became progressively lighter until his was the only vehicle on the road.

He directed his attention to the numbers painted on the mailboxes sitting at the roadside, and soon he saw the one he wanted. The turnoff was nothing more than a gravel track, ending at a ramshackle house a quarter-mile away.

Caden couldn't drive very fast without his front-wheel-drive Ford Fusion skidding on the loose gravel. As he got closer to the house, he noticed that, although dusk was settling, no lights were visible inside it. He saw no vehicles parked where the gravel road ended in front of the house. Torn shades were drawn, partially blocking the view of the darkened interior of the farm house. So far as Caden could see, there was no sign of anyone inside the house. It looked abandoned. But maybe that was what the agents wanted.

Why had Agent Neilson chosen this out-of-the-way place? Maybe the DEA had set up headquarters here for privacy. Perhaps there were cars hidden in back, out of sight. And they would arrange it to look like the farmhouse was deserted. On the other hand, this could be … No. That only happened in the movies or in novels.

He opened the car door and started to get out, but before Caden could fully exit the vehicle he heard a loud crack. Reflex drove him to dive back into the car, sheltering there. That sounded like a shot, but that was impossible. He kept his head below the dashboard while he replayed what had just happened. Was the sound a product of his imagination? Was someone really shooting at him? When the second shot rang out, he raised his head long enough to see dirt fly up a few yards in front of his vehicle. This hadn't felt right, and now he was certain. It was a setup, and it was time for him to get away.

Keeping his head down as best he could, Caden started the car and slammed it into drive. He spun the wheel in the tightest turn he could manage, but it wasn't any easier to drive away on the loose gravel road than it had been to arrive. He heard another gunshot almost simultaneous with a metallic sound as the round hit the trunk of his car. Caden spared a glance into the rearview mirror. No one seemed to be chasing him, but he still wanted to get away from there.

When his car reached the junction of the road with the highway, Caden whipped the car into a tight turn, trying to pick up speed as he transitioned from the loose gravel onto the pavement. His vehicle fishtailed, hitting the mailbox before spinning out of control. While he tried to correct, he heard a loud air horn. That was when he saw a truck coming at him on a collision course.

13

At home, Beth picked up Kitty and held her, taking comfort from the presence of another beating heart in the house. How many times since Caden set up his surgical practice here in Freeman had she been grateful for Kitty's presence. She loved the little kitten, but it was no substitute for Caden ... or for the child they both wanted.

Her thoughts were interrupted by the ring of the phone. At first, she thought it was Caden calling. She had a hundred questions for him, but the main thing was that he was safe. Then she realized it was the landline ringing. Probably someone wanting to sell her a cruise. But when she looked at the caller ID, it showed that the call was from her father-in-law.

"Henry, how are you doing?"

"I'm fine, Beth. I wanted to tell both of you where I am with the workup of my ... my cancer. Is Caden there?"

Beth had brought Kitty with her when she went to the phone. Now she set the kitten down and reached for a pad and pencil. "No, not right now, and I don't know when he's coming home. Can I give him a message? Or we can call back, so you can talk with both of us."

"No need. I just wanted you both to know that I've scheduled my endoscopy with biopsy. Dr. Ross is going to do it tomorrow morning."

She was scribbling as Henry talked. "Do you want one of us to drive you to and from the procedure?"

"No, I've got it taken care of."

Probably with Jean. It was just as well that Caden wasn't here to talk with his father. Beth wasn't certain, but it was possible that her husband was still hanging on to his theory that Jean had in some way contributed to his mother's death. He certainly still resented the role she was taking in his father's life.

"I'll give this information to Caden when he comes in. And will you be at home if he wants to call?"

"I don't think so. I need to go back to my office for a bit. Then I may go over to Jean's."

Beth was thinking about her response when there was a beep that signaled someone else was calling. "I've got another call coming in, Henry. Looks like it's from the emergency room. They may have something for Caden, so I guess I'd better take it."

After promising to talk with Henry later, Beth answered the other call. "This is Mrs. Taggart."

"Beth, it's me. I don't have my cell phone right now, and I practically had to threaten the people here in the ER to get to use their landline. I'm okay, but—"

Caden's conversation was cut off suddenly and replaced by a different male voice. "Beth, this is Jim Sparling. I was in the ER when the paramedics brought Caden in. He's been in an accident. He's okay now, but you probably should come down here."

At the offices of Drs. Henry Taggart and Claude Horner, all the lights were off except a lamp illuminating Dr. Horner's desk. A scratch pad in front of him was filled with figures. The man sat with his head in his hands, occasionally looking up to check a figure, then bowing his head once more.

The office suite had been quiet for a while when Horner heard a noise at the back door. It wasn't the normal sound of a key turning in the lock. It was a series of scratches and thumps. Finally, the door opened and closed.

Horner frowned. There were only a few people with keys to that door, but this didn't sound like someone using one. He had never heard someone pick a lock or jimmy a door to open it, but this was what he imagined it would sound like. It was probably silly, but there'd been a rash of break-ins to medical offices recently. Suppose someone had come through the back door, expecting the suite to be empty?

Although some of his colleagues had guns in their desk for just such an eventuality, Horner didn't. He looked around and realized there was no weapon readily available for him to use. He picked up the phone and had punched in 9-1 when Henry Taggart's head appeared in the doorway.

"Claude. Got a minute?"

"Sure. Come in." Horner returned the receiver to its cradle. Despite the air-conditioning in the office, Claude felt a trickle of sweat beneath his dress shirt. He decided not to tell his partner how his entrance to the building startled him.

"Sorry to make such a noise." Henry smiled. "I tried to make the key to my house work in this lock."

"Have a seat." Horner was wondering how he could find out where his associate had been. While he was deciding, Henry solved the problem for him.

"You remember I told you there's a possibility I might have pancreatic cancer," Henry said.

"Yes. And you put that workup on hold when Nancy died. Are you moving forward now?"

"I'll undergo an endoscopic ultrasound and needle biopsy tomorrow."

"At our hospital? At a surgical center?" Claude asked. "Who's doing it?"

Henry pursed his lips. "I don't really want to talk about the details now. All you need to know is that I'll be out tomorrow. I'll talk with you when the biopsy results are in, and we can make plans for the practice." He rose from his chair. "I hope you understand."

"Sure, Henry. This is a tough situation, and you've made a big decision today. Now you want to put it out of your mind for a few hours." Claude cast a compassionate look at his long-time associate. "But whatever you need, just let me know."

"I will," Henry said. He rose, but before he left the office he turned back to his partner. "Claude, say a prayer for me, will you?"

Claude waited until he heard the door close and the office suite was quiet again. Then he pulled the pad toward him, scratched out some figures and wrote in others. Claude looked off into the middle distance as he ran through everything once more. Then he nodded to himself. He'd need to tell Nelda about this latest development. But just maybe this would all work out for the best. Except for Henry, of course.

Beth found Caden in the ER, his right wrist partially immobilized by a splint from palm to mid-forearm, a bandage covering his forehead. He was sitting on the side of a gurney, arguing with Dr. Sparling.

She was hesitant to do more than give Caden a peck on the cheek until he enfolded her in a full-on embrace. "Don't hurt yourself," she said.

Caden looked at his colleague. "I keep telling Jim I'm fine. The X-rays of this wrist don't show a fracture. And my skull films are negative—just a little forehead laceration, which they closed with butterflies."

"The wrist is sprained, and keeping it braced for a few days will help it heal faster," Sparling said. "As for the bandage on your forehead, you can change it to a smaller one when you get home. But I don't plan to let you go until we see if there's something going on that an X-ray doesn't show us."

"You mean you want to keep me for observation."

Sparling nodded.

"You can't hold me here, Jim." Caden pointed to Beth. "She's a trained nurse. We both know what to watch for in case a subdural hematoma or some other complication starts to develop. And I promise to use the brace for a few days. Now can I go home?"

Sparling looked at his colleague and shrugged. Then he turned to Beth. "They say the Lord watches out for fools and children. I don't know which one this guy is, but to total his car and get out of it with no more than a sprained wrist and a bump on the head tells me that Someone is taking care of him."

Beth nodded her agreement. *And maybe my prayers while he was gone had something to do with it.*

After another twenty minutes, Caden was ready to leave the ER. Sparling looked at him and shook his head. "Just take it easy, and don't worry about the office. We'll see you on Monday, if you feel up to it."

Beth saw her husband open his mouth, but she squeezed his shoulder and shook her head. Miracle of miracles, he seemed to get the message, and remained silent.

She had to almost fight Caden to get him to follow the rules and be rolled in a wheelchair to her car, but at last they were headed home.

"That call I got before I left, the one I thought was from Neilson, didn't come from him," he told her. "This was a setup. Someone took several shots at me. I think the only bullet that got near me went through the trunk of the car. But when I made my getaway I took the turn off the gravel road too fast. I tangled with a truck and lost."

"What happened then?" she said, her eyes fixed on the road.

"The man in the truck used his cell phone to call for help. My phone was on the seat beside me, and it's probably still in the car somewhere. I was trapped until the firemen and paramedics pried me out and sent me to the hospital."

"I'm glad you're okay. And the car?"

"I'm sure it's totaled. You can check with the wrecker service and try to retrieve my phone and stuff tomorrow."

"Did the police talk with you?"

Caden started to nod his head, then stopped. "Ouch. I have pains in some places I didn't anticipate. The police think I was turning onto the highway, lost control, took out a mailbox when I fishtailed, and ended up with that truck T-boning my car." He waited, and when there was no reaction, he went on. "I want to talk with Neilson before I give the police details about the shots that were fired at me."

"Do you have his cell number?"

"Yeah, stored in my cell phone. I guess I'll have to wait to call him until we can retrieve it." He noticed Beth turning on her blinker for a right turn. "Where are you going?"

"Neilson tried to reach you at the office. The caller ID captured the number."

"Great," Caden said.

"Oh, and your father called. He's going ahead with the biopsy. It's scheduled for tomorrow morning. And he apparently has a new doctor. I'll give you all those details after we get home."

Caden sat at the desk in his office. He touched the bandage on his forehead and wished he'd asked for pain medication before he left the hospital. He really hadn't had a lot of discomfort after the accident, but maybe that had been the masking effect of the adrenaline. And that was rapidly wearing off. "Beth, don't we have some Tylenol around here?"

"I'll get it." She left to find the mild pain-reliever for him. Caden knew his colleague had been right—he really shouldn't be moving around right now, but he wanted to contact Neilson. Beth had retrieved the DEA agent's cell phone number from the caller ID at his office, and that was the number he dialed as he waited for medication to help stop the army of little men hammering on his skull.

After five rings, Caden resigned himself to leaving a message. But then the call was answered with a brusque, "Yes?"

"Agent Neilson, this is Dr. Caden Taggart. I wanted to let you—"

"Where have you been? You left a message for me to call you. I tried to, but you didn't answer your cell phone."

"Someone phoned pretending to be you. They sent me to a deserted farm house to set me up for an ambush. I managed to turn my car around but had a wreck as I escaped."

There was silence on the other end of the call. Caden took advantage of the lull to accept two extra-strength Tylenol tablets and a glass of water from Beth.

"I can't talk right now. Can we meet tomorrow morning?"

What day was this? Tomorrow was Friday. Caden didn't remember anything special on his schedule. He'd have to take their one remaining car, but he could make an early meeting with the agent, then double back to pick up Beth. "I think so."

"I'll meet you about a quarter to seven in the hospital coffee shop," Neilson said. "Until then, be careful."

Henry Taggart rolled out of bed at 5:00 a.m. on Friday, ending a night marked by brief naps interspersed with long stretches when he lay in bed with his eyes wide open. His mind was going at warp speed, thinking of what was ahead, knowing he could do nothing about it except be swept along in the process. He'd finally decided that any further attempts at rest were out of the question.

Now he knew how his patients felt before he performed an exploratory laparotomy to determine whether their cancer was operable or not. He'd always tried to reassure them and calm their fears, but he'd never really experienced the anxiety they must feel. Today he did.

Henry remembered something he'd heard in medical school. The professor had talked about anxiety as an unreasonable fear of the unknown. Well, he'd have to challenge that. Sometimes it was just as bad to know as not know. And because he was a doctor, a surgeon, he knew all the things that came after a confirmed diagnosis of carcinoma of the pancreas.

He slid his feet into slippers and padded to the kitchen, stopping halfway there. Henry had been about to flip on the coffee maker, but he couldn't have coffee this morning. He couldn't even have water. Nothing to eat or drink after midnight was the main instruction he'd been given.

Was there anything else he needed to do? He'd been told to stop blood thinners and aspirin, but since he didn't take these, there was no need to discontinue them. He had mild hypertension, easily controlled with one pill a day. He could take that with a small sip of water, the nurse told him.

Henry wondered if he might cheat and perhaps have a sip of black coffee instead of water with his pill. Ever since he was in medical school he'd run on coffee, and that habit stayed with him through the years. Surely a sip wouldn't hurt anything. After several seconds of deliberation, he reluctantly decided it was best to do exactly what the doctor ordered. He'd always heard that doctors were the worst patients. Right now, he tended to agree.

He took his time shaving and dressing. When he opened the front door, it was still dark outside, but the newspaper was already on his porch. He brought it inside and began browsing through it, but when he came to the obituaries, Henry closed the paper and put it aside. That was too much a reminder of his mortality.

He looked at the clock in the kitchen. He needed to be at the outpatient center, the place where Dr. Ross would perform the endoscopy and biopsy, at 6:00 a.m. He'd arranged to be picked up at his house this morning by a taxi. He intended to go home the same way after his procedure. The nurse he talked with at the outpatient center had argued with him, warning that he'd be a bit woozy from his IV sedation, which is why they required a responsible individual be with the patient afterward.

"I'm a doctor. I've arranged my transportation, and I'll be able to care for myself at home."

It took quite a bit of arguing, but eventually he had convinced them. Now he wished he hadn't been so stubborn.

He wasn't totally certain why he'd decided to keep Jean out of the process. Maybe it was to prove he could handle this on his own. Or perhaps he was afraid he'd become a bit too dependent on her. The loss of his wife was still fresh enough that Henry felt a little guilt because there was another woman sharing some aspects of his life. He wasn't ready to compound that.

When his son called him back late last night, Henry told him he was going ahead with the biopsy this morning. Caden volunteered to drive there and ferry him back and forth for the procedure but received the same response that he had given the nurse at the outpatient surgery center. He had it covered. *I don't want them making a fuss over me. They have busy lives of their own.* Actually, Henry realized he didn't want to feel dependent on someone else—not on Caden or Beth or Jean. Not on anyone.

If the biopsy showed what both consultants predicted, was Henry ready to commit suicide? And would he ask Caden for help in doing that? Lots had happened since that initial conversation he had with his son. Was he still ready to take his own life before the cancer did? Some people survived—lived for years. Could he be one of them? The odds of beating this were slim, but they weren't zero. Did he want to take the risk? At least he'd found that if his death was the result of a suicide, his life insurance would still pay off.

He looked at his watch. The taxi would be here in about fifteen more minutes. He didn't want to pick up a book. The newspaper was out. Henry had no desire to turn on the TV. He wandered into the study, eased into what he considered "his" chair, and closed his eyes. He wished he had a do-over on so many parts of his life. But it was too late to change what had gone before.

Finally, Henry stretched out his hand and pulled the leather-bound Bible off the coffee table. It hadn't been opened since Nancy's stroke, but thanks to once-a-week cleaning by the maid there was no dust on the book or around it. He let it fall open, hoping he'd find a note that Nancy had left in the margin. He'd give anything to see her handwriting again. But instead of a note he saw a passage she had highlighted with a yellow marker: "God is our refuge and strength, a very present help in time of trouble."

Henry recalled the times he'd found Nancy sitting in this room reading this same Bible. Then, in a rush, more memories came flooding back—memories of her encouraging him to accompany his family to church instead of making hospital rounds or playing golf. He recalled the gentle way she'd tried to get him to open his heart to the Author of this book. But he'd put her off, again and again. Was it time for him to take that step now?

He was still sitting there, the Bible open in his lap, when the taxi pulled up outside and honked.

14

Caden stirred sweetener into what would be his third cup of coffee for that Friday morning and looked around. The crowd hitting the hospital's food court about this time swirled around him, but he didn't see Neilson. He looked down at his watch. The agent was fifteen minutes late. He'd give him another ten, but then Caden needed to go home and pick up Beth. Today he wanted to see about a rental car, maybe buy a new one if his little Ford was indeed totaled.

The scrape of a chair to his immediate right made him turn in that direction. Neilson was out of uniform, so to speak—no suit and tie today. He wore chinos and a golf shirt, covered by a dark blue jacket.

"I was about to give up."

Neilson put down the cup of coffee and sweet roll he carried. He took a sip of the hot liquid before speaking. "I had to navigate a traffic tie-up on my way." He lifted the pastry, took a bite, and chewed slowly. Neilson waited until he'd swallowed and chased it with more coffee. "Tell me about this incident yesterday."

"You might call it an incident. I call it a near-death experience," Caden said. Then, while Neilson polished off his sweet roll and finished his coffee, he related the whole story—the phone call with voice recognition made difficult by static, the apparently deserted farmhouse, the rifle shots that sent him hurrying away, and the crash that ended the story.

"And one of the shots hit your car's trunk?"

"It sounded like that to me."

"What did you tell the police?" Neilson asked.

"They think I came out of the gravel road too fast, skidded, and hit the truck."

"Did you say anything about the shots? Do you think they noticed the bullet hole in the trunk?"

Caden thought about that. "No. They gave me a ticket, and a flat-bed wrecker came for my car."

Neilson pulled a small notebook from the inside pocket of his jacket, clicked a ballpoint pen, and made a note. "If your car isn't drivable, I presume it's still at the lot where the tow truck took it."

"I haven't checked yet, but I suppose it is."

"I'll take a look," Neilson said.

"If you or Harwell go out there today, look for my cell phone in the car. I had it beside me, using it for directions to this place, and I imagine it slid onto the floorboard or under the seat with the crash."

"Better get another one," Neilson said. "I may need to keep that one for a bit."

"Why?"

"Did it ever occur to you that it might be helpful for me to know the number that called you and arranged what you call a setup?"

"Won't work," Caden said. "Caller ID didn't show the identity of the caller."

"Leave it to me," Neilson said. "There are ways." And with that, he pushed back his chair and soon was lost in the crowd that continued to swirl around the food court.

When she heard the car pull up in the driveway and honk twice, Beth drained the last of her coffee, put the cup and saucer in the sink, and headed out. She picked up her purse and coat, made sure the door locked behind her, and slid into the front seat of their Subaru Outback. She had barely fastened her seat belt before Caden backed out of the drive and headed for the office.

"How was the meeting with Agent Neilson?"

Caden didn't take his eyes off the road. "Unsatisfactory. I told him all about the incident last night. I expected him to tell me he was winding up his investigation, maybe reveal who was doing what, but instead it was another one-way street. He got some information from me and hurried out of there."

"Do you think you should go to the police?"

"I've been thinking about that. But the DEA agents have told me they want to keep this investigation quiet, and we all know that the more people who know about anything, the greater the chance of a leak. I'm going to give it just a bit longer."

"I don't know why," Beth said. "You've had anonymous phone calls, been shot at, been in a car wreck. The next time the people responsible reach out, you may end up dead."

Caden didn't respond to that. Just maintained the grim expression he'd had since his meeting with Agent Neilson.

Henry Taggart regained consciousness slowly. It wasn't a sudden thing, like someone throwing open the curtains to view the day outside. He'd been wrapped in a dreamless sleep from which he gradually emerged like the slow fade-in of a movie. When he finally had his senses about him, he looked around and saw he was in the recovery room.

It took a few seconds, maybe a full minute, before he realized his procedure was finished. *I guess I should be happy. Didn't I want to get this over?* No, what he wanted was for the procedure not to be necessary in the first place. But it had to be done—two consultants had told him that. And no matter how much he wanted to ignore it, his problem wasn't going away. Well, now the die was cast. There was nothing more to do but wait for the verdict, then move on.

"Awake? You had a nice nap, thanks to some IV Versed."

Henry looked to the right and saw Dr. Ross standing next to where he lay. The doctor was in scrubs, a cap still covering his hair. He moved closer to Henry and spoke in a low voice. "I found exactly what the other studies suggested. You have a solid mass behind the first part of your small intestine."

"The C-loop of the duodenum," Henry said.

"Right. I guess I'm used to talking in layman's terms. Anyway, I took several needle biopsies. I think the odds are high that the mass is a carcinoma of the pancreas. But if it is, we caught it early, so don't immediately expect the worst."

Henry didn't feel particularly grateful at the moment, but he knew Dr. Ross was trying to be upbeat with him. "Thanks."

Ross looked around. "I'll go out to the waiting room and tell the family. One or two of them should be able to come in here and see you soon."

"I ... I came by taxi. I plan to go home the same way."

"That's not what we ask," Ross said. "You need to have a driver who brings you and takes you home. You'll be sleepy, and—"

Henry held up a hand, the one not encumbered by an IV. "Look, Dr. Ross. I have my reasons. I finally convinced the lady who gave me my instructions to let me do this. I'll let my family know—my son is a doctor—and I'm capable of taking care of myself at home. If it makes you feel any better, there's a nurse I can call if I need anyone."

Ross threw up his hands. "If you weren't a doctor—"

"Thank you. I'll be fine."

"Any questions?" Ross asked, almost as an afterthought.

Henry shook his head. Oh, he had questions, all right, but he knew there was no need to ask them because there were no answers—at least, not yet.

"We'll talk more when I get the biopsies back. Then we can discuss where we go from here. I'll be back later to check on you again."

Henry didn't reply. He knew there were several things that could be done, things that might stretch his life by a few months, maybe even a year or two, possibly more. Then again, there was always the possibility that long before that time was up he would meet death on his own terms. He hadn't completely made up his mind.

He rolled over and tried to get back to sleep, but he was too keyed up. His mind flitted hither and yon, settling for a moment on each of his worries and then moving on. Finally, he recalled the words he'd read earlier that morning.

"God is our refuge and strength, a very present help in time of trouble." At that point, he closed his eyes and tried to turn off his mind. What had Nancy said on more than one occasion? "Let go and let God."

Driving to the office on Friday with Beth beside him, Caden found his sprained wrist didn't bother him so long as he wore the splint to support it. Once he reached the office he decided doctors weren't supposed to show weakness, so he removed the splint and replaced the taped-on bandage on his forehead with a large, flesh-colored Band-Aid.

As soon as he started down the hall for his office, Rose met him with a cup of coffee. Beth had slipped into her role so well, he'd almost forgotten about Rose, but her first words brought him back to reality in a hurry.

She set the coffee cup on his desk and waited until he was seated. "Dr. Taggart, I know this isn't a good time for you, especially with your dad's surgery and your car accident, but I need to tell you this. I've wanted to for a day or two, but—"

"That's okay, Rose. Just tell me."

"My husband's transfer has been moved up. And it would really help if I could make this my last day." Rose looked as though she expected him to explode, but Caden didn't.

"If we'd had a bit more warning—"

"No, I understand. But Beth is doing a good job, so you aren't going to be caught short-handed."

Rose promised to let Beth and the other nurses know this would be her last day. Just before she exited his office, she turned toward him and said, "Thank you." Then she was gone.

Caden made it through the morning with no problems except a brief argument with Jim Sparling about coming to work so soon. He did sneak off and take a couple of extra-strength Tylenol tabs after the first patient. When he passed Beth in the hall, she gave him a wink and a nod. Rose had apparently told her the news, and she was letting him know she was ready to take over. Caden breathed a sigh of relief.

He was supposed to be off on Friday afternoon, but that only meant a change of scenery, not a time to put his feet up and rest. His first call was to his insurance agent, who promised an adjustor would check out his wrecked car within the next day or so. In the meantime, just rent a car and they'd work out the details later.

Then Caden called a friend at a local car dealership. Caden had acquired his now-wrecked Ford Fusion as a used car and had driven it through med school and residency. He didn't know the exact mileage it had on it, but it had to be well over 250 thousand. Maybe he should go ahead and trade it in.

"See what your insurance company will give you for your car, and we should be able to make a deal. In the meantime, let me arrange a rental car for you."

It wasn't long before the paperwork was done for the rental. Caden kissed Beth good-bye, and she left in the Outback to run her own errands. Now he was ready to tackle more of his to-do list.

One of the first things Caden did after getting the rental car, a Toyota Camry, was to throw the wrist brace into the back seat. He hated using it. He'd almost prefer a little discomfort to answering all the questions the brace generated.

His father had said he was to undergo the endoscopy with biopsy this morning. With the IV sedation, Henry would be sleepy most of the day, but maybe there was a way to check on him without waking him up. Yes, there was. But it meant calling Jean, and Caden didn't want to do that. He'd wait and call his father's number later this afternoon.

Meanwhile, Caden needed a new cell phone, so he headed for the phone store. Neilson told him to get another phone, as though it were the easiest thing in the world. But Caden dreaded having to choose one. Maybe whoever helped him pick one out would take pity on his lack of sophistication.

Like some men, Caden felt that the instruction book in the glove compartment of his rental car was a last resort. He alternated between watching where he was driving and glancing at the various switches and knobs. Then, as he approached an intersection controlled by four-way stop signs, Caden noticed just in time that a pickup on his right cruised right past the sign, causing him to slam on the brakes in a panic stop.

He sat there at the intersection until the driver behind him honked. Caden pulled forward slowly, turning his head to look in all directions at once. Maybe he'd better save the familiarization until a time when he wasn't moving.

Once again, Henry awoke groggy. Was this some sort of *déjà vu*? He tried to remember where he was. Then he opened his eyes, looked around him, and realized he was no longer in the recovery room. No, he was in his home, stretched out on the living room couch.

How did he get here? What time was it? Matter of fact, what day was it? Then he began to piece it together. He'd undergone a procedure with biopsy that morning. The anesthesiologist had started an IV and administered "something to relax him." He remembered waking up in the recovery room at the outpatient center. He remembered talking with the doctor. After that, things got a little blurry, but he was eventually able to recall climbing into a wheelchair and rolling out to the taxi waiting at the curb.

Had he paid the taxi driver? Yes, he did. After the man, who insisted on walking him to the door, had gone, Henry vaguely remembered collapsing onto the couch. Now his watch showed it was four o'clock. Was that morning or afternoon? Still lying on the couch, he turned to look through the slit in the partially opened drapes. Bright sun was visible outside, so it must be four in the afternoon. He'd slept for almost half a day.

Why hadn't he let Jean drive him home? She would have been happy to provide transportation, fix him some food, help him get into bed, take care of him. Oh, yes. He'd made the decision not to involve Jean because Nancy was dead, and he wasn't ready for Jean or any other woman to take over her role. He wanted to be independent.

The buzz of his cell phone caused him to come a little more awake. That was one of the penalties of being a doctor—a ringing phone produced an immediate reaction, whatever the state that preceded it. He followed the vibration and found his cell stuck between two of the sofa cushions.

He fumbled it out and punched the button to answer the call. "Dr. Taggart."

"Henry, this is Jean. Are you okay?"

Henry tried to sit up. His first effort made him dizzy, but on trying again he found that by doing it slowly he could make it to an upright position without falling over. "I'm fine. Just waking up from a nap."

"I wondered why you weren't at work today. No one seemed to know. Eventually, I asked Dr. Horner, who hemmed and hawed. What he finally said was that you were taking care of some personal business."

"I ... I guess that's one way to put it."

"Henry, are you okay? You sound groggy."

He started to shake his head, then thought better of it. "No, no. As I told you, I took a nap and your call woke me. I'm fine."

"I think there's something you're not telling me," Jean said. "I'd better come over there and we can talk about this ... whatever it is."

Henry thought for a moment. He was being silly, and now was the time to set things right. "Give me half an hour to shower and change. Come on over and I'll tell you everything."

15

It had been several hours since Beth had driven away from the dealership where Caden planned to pick up a loaner car. She figured that by now he'd had enough time to go by the cell phone store. She tried his "old" cell phone number, but the call went unanswered. Would his new cell phone have the same number? She wasn't certain. With a sigh, she put down the phone and decided she had no alternative but to wait.

Beth had come to the same conclusion as Caden did. If she wanted to get a report on Henry's procedure today, calling Jean provided the best option. And it was probably up to her to make the call. Beth dialed that number and waited through six rings before the call rolled over to voicemail. Maybe Jean had accompanied Henry for the test, and if they were still at the hospital she might not have turned on her phone.

Her cell phone rang while it was still in her hand, and she answered it. Beth hoped Caden had picked up a new phone, and possibly had a different number as a result. Sure enough, when she looked at the caller ID, she didn't recognize the number. But with Caden gone, she decided to answer it.

"Hello?"

"Beth, it's me. Let me assure you that I'm all right."

When she heard Caden's voice, she relaxed, but when his second sentence hit her ears her heart lodged firmly in her throat. "What happened?"

"I was getting ready to back out of my parking space at the cell phone store when someone came around the corner and clipped the rear of my car. It didn't do much damage to the rental car I was driving, but the other vehicle looks like it's been in a fight and lost—crumpled right front fender, good-sized dent in the passenger door."

Beth realized she'd been holding her breath. "But you're okay."

"I'm fine, but someone saw the wreck and called the police. My new cell phone isn't activated yet, so I'm borrowing a phone to call you."

"Is there anything I can do?"

"No. Now let me make one more call before the police get here."

Beth frowned. "Who?

"My attorney. I think I need to involve the police in all this, and I want to make sure he agrees."

"I'm sure he will," Beth said. "I don't care what the DEA agents asked. And stay in touch."

No sooner had Beth put down the phone than it rang. She looked and saw that Jean was calling her back.

"I was talking with Henry when you called," Jean said.

"Is he okay? I understand he was supposed to have an endoscopy and biopsy today."

"I guess he did. I didn't find out about it until earlier today."

"I don't understand," Beth said. "Haven't you usually been the one to drive him to these appointments?"

"Yes, until this one. I phoned him just a few minutes ago. He finally said if I come over in about half an hour, he'd tell me all about it."

"Why—"

"Why wouldn't he let me be there with him?" Jean said. "I can think of a couple of reasons. Maybe he thought that after Nancy died he was being too dependent on me. Perhaps he thought I was auditioning for the role of Mrs. Henry Taggart."

"I hope not," Beth said, although she knew Caden had that very thought. Matter of fact, he still harbored the opinion that Jean had a hand in Nancy Taggart's death. Had Henry come around to that way of thinking, as well?

Jean responded. "Maybe he decided to be all *macho* and get through this without my help. I don't know."

"Well, let me know what you find out," Beth said.

Caden thought back over what might have been the modern version of a Greek tragedy—one that included an attempt by a person or persons unknown to kill him. He'd made what in retrospect was a mistake when he initially passed on hiring an attorney to protect his interests, instead blindly trying to cooperate with the DEA agents who showed up in his office.

Someone, impersonating one of those men on the phone, had lured him—no better word for it—had lured him to an abandoned farm house where he'd almost been shot. Now he was jumping at shadows, couldn't pin down the agents (who'd by and large disappeared), and now he was at the police station, waiting to talk with a detective.

His attorney had agreed with the action he was taking, summing it up by saying, "It's about time." Caden had turned down Mel Sewell's offer to come to the station, promising to call him if this turned into more than just his giving a bare statement to the police detective.

"Remember, don't hesitate to call me. And if you do, don't say anything more until I get there."

"You Dr. Taggart?"

Caden looked up from his seat near the desk sergeant at a stout man in his mid-50s. He wore a suit that was from one of the lower end stores. His white shirt was clean, his tie conservative if you ignored the small gravy spot on it. But what really gave him away as a detective were the thick-soled shoes and the look that he'd seen it all and believed little, if any, of it.

"That's me." Caden rose.

"Detective Caruso." He offered a handshake that was firm without any attempt to be overpowering. "Let's go back to my office. I understand you've had an interesting several days, and you want to talk about it."

Beth was reading. At least, she held a book on her lap and tried to make sense of the words, but she couldn't concentrate. Instead, she found herself wondering about Caden. She was certain her husband wasn't involved in any scheme to prescribe drugs to fictitious patients. Yes, it made sense that someone had gotten hold of his DEA number. On her first day at work she'd seen how easy it would be for someone to use the credentials of any of the three doctors practicing in that office. She couldn't believe Caden was a part of this.

But he apparently *was* involved in it, although Beth didn't know why. Why did the person making the anonymous phone calls about the DEA investigators choose to warn Caden? Why did someone lure him to a deserted farmhouse and try to kill him. Why were they—whoever "they" were—intent on taking him out of the game?

Beth started, dropping her book on her lap, when she heard the front door open and close.

"I'm home," Caden called. "Finally."

"I'm glad." The kiss Beth gave her husband was more tender than usual, the hug lasted longer. "I'm glad you're safe. I'm glad you're here. And I'll be glad when this is over."

"That makes two of us." Caden followed Beth into the living room and virtually collapsed onto the sofa. "I have a rental car, even though it has a dent in the rear bumper. They offered me another one, but I've traded cars enough today."

"How was your time with the police?"

Caden sighed. "Mel Sewell agreed with me that it was time to involve them, so I followed the patrolman to the police station. I've spent the past hour talking with Detective Caruso. And you know what? I feel better. I should have gone to my lawyer first when the DEA agents approached me. Now I'm glad the police know about all this, and I wish I'd shared events with them sooner as well."

"The main thing is you're home—safe," Beth said.

He squeezed her hand. "What have you found out about my dad's biopsy?"

Henry steadied himself with one hand against the door frame as he turned the knob and opened the door for Jean. "Come in."

She followed him into his study, the room where he seemed to spend most of his time after Nancy's death. At least, that was where they'd sat and talked the few times she'd seen him outside of work since then.

Henry lowered himself into the recliner that sat in the corner—"his" chair, as she'd heard him refer to it—and nodded to her. "Thank you for coming over.

"I'd have done a lot more if you let me. Why didn't you tell me you were having the biopsy? I would have driven you there and back, taken care of anything you needed while you recovered from the anesthetic—"

"Yes. You would have done what my wife would have," Henry said. "While Nancy was alive, you were simply a friend, helping out. But now that she's … Now that she's gone, I realized that people might think you were auditioning for the role she filled."

"You mean your son might take it that way."

"What Caden thinks is important to me, Jean."

She shook her head. "Henry, I've known you for more than a decade. You stood by me when my husband was killed in a car crash, and you didn't seem to care what other people might think about it. You were simply a friend, and that's what I needed at that time. Why is this different?"

Henry was silent for several seconds. "I don't know."

"I do," Jean said. "I don't think it's necessarily because of what other people might think. I think it's because of the feelings you're noticing, feelings that have surfaced now that you're not—" She paused, weighing her words. "I'll go ahead and say it. You're not encumbered by Nancy. And those may be normal feelings, Henry. But they don't mean either of us needs to act on them. Because they may change."

He smiled. "You've been around me too long, Jean. You're beginning to be as direct as I am sometimes. What I hear you saying is that it's okay for me to lean on you while I find out ... while I find out what's ahead for me."

"It's okay for me to be a friend. That's what you need right now, and that's what I'll be—that's all I'll be."

Caden made the same bedtime rounds of the house he always did, but he took a bit more care with each door and window, making sure they were closed and locked. As he went by the large window in the living room, he pulled the drapes aside and peeped outside to make certain there were no unfamiliar vehicles parked on the street. When he was satisfied things were as they should be, he double-checked to make certain the drapes were fully closed.

He and Beth had stayed up later than usual, hoping that either Henry or Jean would call to report on how his procedure went that day. Finally, Caden said, "If something went wrong, we would have heard by now. Let's get some sleep."

As he was crawling into bed, he was startled by the ringing of the landline. A glance at the bedside clock told him it was almost midnight. Was it the ER? He wasn't on call. His father? He rarely called—or, at least, not until the diagnosis of pancreatic carcinoma had been suggested—and when he did, it was always in the early part of the evening. However, maybe he'd let time slip away from him and didn't want to neglect telling his son and daughter-in-law about his procedure. Caden hoped that was the case.

He picked up the receiver and answered. But it wasn't the hospital. Nor was his father on the other end of the call. Once more he heard the electronically modified voice deliver a message that burned itself into his brain.

"Don't believe anything the DEA agents tell you."

16

Because it was Saturday, and Caden had no patients in the hospital, he and Beth were sitting at the breakfast table, talking and enjoying their second or third cup of coffee—Caden had lost count. They'd long since finished breakfast. They'd read the paper. And eventually they got around to talking about the elephant in the room—Caden's father's biopsy, the DEA agents, and the attempt on Caden's life. Their conversation was interrupted by the ringing of the phone.

"You're not on call, are you?" Beth asked.

"No, Jim Sparling has it this weekend."

"He seems to be taking call a lot."

Caden reached for the phone. "Jim's trying to build up his practice. If you'll recall, I was where he is just a few years ago. I was a poor boy, just getting started." He lifted the receiver. "Hello?"

"Caden, I'm sorry I didn't call you yesterday."

He recognized his father's voice and signaled to Beth. "I'm glad to hear from you, Dad. Let me put this on speaker. Beth is right here."

There was a short pause before she said, "How did the procedure go yesterday?"

"No problems. As I was saying, I'm sorry I let the day get away from me yesterday. I was sort of sleepy from the Versed they gave me, then I talked with Jean for a while, and after that I went back to sleep."

"What did your doctor find?" Caden asked.

"Dr. Ross said things looked about as he expected. He took some needle biopsies, and he'll call me when the path report comes back."

"Are you doing okay?"

"I'm fine."

Beth leaned toward the phone. "Is there anything we can do?"

"No," Henry replied. "I'm just taking it easy today. I'll let you know when the biopsy reports come back. Then I guess I need to decide whether I'll go forward with treatment, or just—"

"Dad! No! Let me know what Dr. Ross says, and we'll talk about our next move."

Henry's voice was soft, but there was no mistaking the iron fist under the velvet glove. "There's no *our* to this, son. There's only *my*. It's my life. My cancer. And I'll decide what to do."

Caden opened his mouth to speak, but Beth stopped him with a hand gesture. Instead, she said, "We're glad you're doing okay. Be certain to keep us posted."

After the call was over, Caden looked at his wife. "My father can be the most stubborn creature on the face of this earth."

"But he's still your father," Beth said. "This isn't easy for him, especially the waiting. You have to hold off on trying to convince him to undergo treatment until we see what treatment is possible."

Caden sighed. "You're right, of course. There's no use trying to convince my father of anything until we see what can be done. Surgery is usually the first option, but his tumor may be better treated with radiation or chemotherapy. And there's always the chance that his cancer may be beyond treatment."

"If that's the case..."

"Then we're back to what my father discussed with me in his original call."

Before the conversation could go further, the phone rang again. Caden frowned. "We're really popular this morning."

"Maybe it's that detective. But I doubt he's gotten very far in such a short time." Caden picked up the phone and answered.

"Dr. Taggart, this is Agent Neilson. I need to see you. Where do you want to meet?"

The offices of Drs. Taggart and Horner were closed for the weekend. There was no activity in the building except in the office of Claude Horner. He sat behind his desk, and his wife, Nelda, had pulled up a chair to sit beside him.

Claude pointed to a row of figures with the blunt end of a pen. "This is how much an audit of the books will show we're short."

Nelda studied the figures on the sheet, then whistled silently. "That's a lot."

"Thank you for not asking the obvious question about how this happened or why."

"No need. What's done is done. Now tell me about how this can go away."

Claude unlocked one of his desk drawers and pulled a multi-page document out. "This is mine, but he has the same one." He spread it on the desk, and again using the blunt end of a pen, pointed out some features, ending with the number at the top of the first page.

"One million dollars," Nelda said.

"One million dollars," Claude echoed. "And with that, all my troubles go away."

"Is this going to happen?"

"It's extremely likely. Matter of fact, I guess you'd say you can bank on it."

"No," Nelda said. "You'd better bank on it."

Mid-morning on Saturday, Caden sat in a small coffee shop on the opposite side of town from his office and the hospital where he worked. He occupied the furthest table from the door. His coffee sat untouched before him as his eyes constantly assessed the few people in the establishment. Every few moments, he'd check the time. Where was Neilson? And what was this meeting about?

As he looked at his watch once more, Neilson slid into the chair opposite him. Caden tried to keep a tight hold on his anger, but his words were clipped. "This is the second time you've met me without your partner. Where's Harwell?"

"That's what I want to talk about," Neilson said.

"Then tell me. I'm tired of your phone calls and secret meetings." He moved his coffee cup around the table, making interlocking circles with the spilled beverage.

Neilson looked at Caden, then dropped his eyes to the tabletop. "You need to keep this to yourself. To begin with, we don't think you've been actively involved with the narcotics prescriptions showing up in Freeman."

"You've told me this before. I know I'm innocent. What else?"

"There's a lot more you don't know." As he talked, Neilson plucked a couple of napkins from the dispenser and wiped up the spilled coffee. "As I've said, Harwell and I were sent here from the Seattle office to investigate the flood of false prescriptions showing up in Freeman. Most of them had the DEA number of three doctors—the ones in your group."

Caden held up his hand, palm out. "It's not a group. I own the building, and the other two doctors pay me a sum each month that covers overhead and rent. It's a loose confederation. We share call and help each other out, but we're not tied together as a group."

"Okay, I get your point, but let's look at it this way. There's one computer used by all the nurses to send e-prescriptions for all the drugs the doctors prescribe. It would be fairly easy for anyone in your office suite to send out false narcotics prescriptions every once in a while, using one of the DEA numbers of the physicians. If you're careful and only write a small number of false prescriptions each week, whoever's behind this can clear a significant amount of money without anyone ever catching on."

"Isn't that risky? And what's a 'significant amount'?"

"The risk is low if you don't get greedy and keep the number of scripts within reason. As for money, it varies geographically. Remember those figures I quoted at our first meeting? The maximum prescription for Vicodin and similar narcotics is eight a day for a month, or 240 tabs."

"Yes."

"One of those tablets is worth anywhere from $10 to $40 on the street. A prescription for 240 means between two thousand and ten thousand dollars. Maybe you decide to play it safe and do one script a week. That could yield up to half a million dollars a year. Two scripts, a cool million. Even after paying off anyone else involved, that would be a nice little supplement to an income."

Caden pursed his lips in a silent whistle. "I had no idea how much those prescriptions were worth. But what does that have to do with Harwell, and why he's not here?"

"We were sent here to unmask the person behind the ring that's passing these illicit prescriptions. But I was also instructed to keep an eye on Harwell."

"Why?"

"Because the people at DEA headquarters think he may be involved in this and possibly several other groups that are selling illicit prescriptions for opioids."

Fall weather being what it is in north Texas, the cool wind of yesterday had given way to a mild southerly breeze and the warmth of the sun today. White sails dotted the lake in front of them as Beth sat beside her husband at a picnic table, enjoying lunch. It would be a relaxing moment for most people, but her husband wasn't relaxed. They were well away from any possible listening ears, so she'd encouraged Caden to tell her what he'd learned that morning. And it shocked her.

"I had no idea opioids brought such a high price," she said.

"Some more than others, but Neilson says that even writing one prescription a week for something like hydrocodone or oxycodone can bring in half a million a year. Two per week—"

"A cool million, and Neilson is not only checking up on illicit prescriptions, but also keeping his eyes open for evidence that would incriminate Harwell?"

"That's what he told me," Caden said. "And he asked me to keep it quiet."

Beth put down the remnants of the sandwich she'd been nibbling and wiped her hands on a napkin. "That's the part that bothers me."

"Me too. I don't know if I believe anything or anyone right now. Mel Sewell pointed out how gullible I was to accept the *bona fides* of Neilson and Harwell the first time they appeared in my office. Just because they flashed some IDs and said they were from the DEA, I believed them. I don't trust anyone now. That's why I told all this to the detective yesterday."

"Any word from him? What's his name?"

Caden picked up a plastic glass and drained the iced tea. "Caruso. Not yet. But it feels good to let someone else from law enforcement in on what the DEA agents are doing at my office." He set down the glass. "But I only found out about Harwell this morning, so the detective doesn't know that."

Beth crumpled her paper napkin and stuffed it in her empty plastic glass. "I suppose I can see Nielson's point about not bringing in anyone else on this part of the investigation, but what if he's lying?"

"On any or all of it." He started putting the remnants of lunch back in the hamper. "I'd better keep Caruso informed, and I trust he'll do the same for me." Caden moved items around so he could fit everything in the basket. "I'll be glad when this is over, so I can go back to a normal life."

"That's not going to happen for a while," Beth cautioned. "Let the authorities handle this. You need to focus on your father's diagnosis."

"I guess you're right. And I still think Jean's trying to worm her way into his life. That way, when he dies she'll be able to live like a doctor's rich widow." Caden closed the lid of the picnic hamper with a bit more force than necessary. "And despite my father's refusal to believe it, or even allow an investigation, I still think Jean had a hand in killing my mother."

Before Beth could speak, Caden's cell phone rang. He pulled it from his pocket and glanced at the caller ID. "I don't recognize this. But with things the way they are, I guess I'd better answer it."

The conversation was short, and the part Beth heard gave her no clue as to its content. But when Caden ended the call, she noticed his expression had changed—and not for the better.

17

"When was this discovered?" Caden's voice was remarkably calm as he addressed the two policemen standing just outside the yellow crime scene tape that barred the entrance to his professional building.

The firemen leaving the site seemed to pay no attention to the small group's conversation. They continued to stow the three extinguishers they carried on the large truck behind Caden. Its diesel engine idled, producing a low, thrumming noise that made it necessary for him to speak loudly to the police officer with two stripes on his sleeve. Beth leaned closer to hear. "I said, when was this discovered? And by whom?"

"Our unit was driving by when we heard the smoke alarm blaring. As we got closer, we could see a wisp of smoke coming from underneath the front door, which was unlocked when we checked it."

"Anyone inside when you got here?"

"No, sir. We notified the fire department, and they were able to put out the flames with hand-held extinguishers before it spread beyond a very limited area."

At that moment, a fireman with Captain on his helmet walked up and addressed Caden. "Are you the man who owns this building."

"Yes." Caden offered his hand, but the fireman showed his own hands covered in soot.

"Captain Higgins. I serve as one of the arson investigators for the department." He pointed at the building. "The fire seems to have been confined to your record room, and it's out now. Would you like to look around and tell me if anything else has been affected by the fire?"

Beth had been standing next to Caden, and when she started to follow him in, the captain stopped her. "Sorry, ma'am. No civilians in here right now."

Caden turned around. "She's my wife. She's also a nurse here and may be able to spot something I might miss."

The fireman nodded. He and the patrolman ducked under the yellow "crime scene" tape, leading the way. Caden stopped at the front door. "This door was unlocked when you arrived?"

"Yes, sir."

Caden thought about pursuing that fact, but decided he'd look at what the arsonist had done first.

Beth followed Caden inside, through the undamaged reception room and past the door that led to the record room. When she first started work here, she had noticed that one room stored the records for every doctor, and decided it made sense to have them all in one location. Of course, the practice had switched to electronic medical records after less than a year, so the ones left here were primarily those of inactive patients. And those were the ones that burned. All the others were stored in the "Cloud."

The fire in the records room seemed to have been started by pulling out a couple of dozen or so folders, piling them on the floor next to the open shelves that held the remaining records, and setting them afire. About forty records in all had been partially or completely consumed and others scorched and covered with white foam. Beth hoped these were indeed patients who hadn't been seen in the past year or two.

She moved to the far corner of the room where a communal computer was utilized by all the nurses. When she entered her password, she was pleased to find the machine operating normally, undamaged by the flames and smoke. She recalled a few names from recent appointments, and when she entered them, Beth heaved a sigh of relief as each patient's record came up on the screen.

"What do you think?" Caden asked when Beth returned to where the small group stood near the now-extinguished fire.

"All the active and recent records seem okay. Just some of the folders for inactives appear to be burned."

"Why would someone set such a localized fire?" Caden said.

The fire captain said, "It's a good way to burn down the whole building. If the fire had spread and gotten hotter, the sprinklers would have come on and ruined the contents of your whole office. I talked with the patrolman here, and we both think the front door lock wasn't picked. Someone used a key to get in, pulled records off the shelf, and set them on fire." He picked up a charred file and sniffed it. "The perp probably used an accelerant such as lighter fluid.

Then, when the fire got going, the smoke alarm went off. I suspect whoever it was decided not to stick around, fearing the noise would bring someone, so they got out of here, leaving the front door unlocked."

"We'll check the security cameras in the neighborhood," the senior patrolman said. He turned to Caden. "I don't see cameras anywhere in the office. Do you have any?"

"No, but I'm thinking of installing them now. I'm still puzzled why someone would do this."

"That's what we need to find out." Detective Caruso stood in the doorway. "Doctor, let's go to your office and talk."

Before Beth could say anything, Caruso continued. "And since your wife is a nurse here, I'd like her to come as well."

Caden and Beth settled into seats in his office, with Detective Caruso behind the desk. He took a notepad from the pocket of his wrinkled sport coat, then searched for a pen and finally found one in his shirt pocket. "I doubt you set fire in your own suite, but let's start with where you two have been since about ten o'clock this morning."

Caden looked at Beth, then shrugged. "I got back home about mid-morning. Since it's the weekend, my wife thought this would be a nice day to have a picnic lunch. We were at the lake when I got the call about the fire."

Caruso frowned. "In other words, you and your wife alibi each other, but no one else can corroborate your stories." He scribbled a few words. "And you came right here?"

"I called my attorney, who didn't think there was a need for him to accompany me, but said he'd stand by for my call afterward," Caden said.

"You don't think—" Beth started.

" 'Where were you?' is always going to be our first question. Don't worry. We'll ask other people their whereabouts too. And I suspect most of them won't have an alibi either."

"What do you make of the police finding the front door open when they got here?" Caden asked.

"There was no evidence of forced entry. I assume the perpetrator left in a hurry when the smoke alarm went off. My thought is this is most likely the work of someone who has a key," Caruso replied. "Who had them?"

Caden started ticking off on his fingers all the people who possessed keys, listing each of the doctors, all their nurses, and the two receptionists. "We never thought about security. Only convenience. We may have to rethink all that."

"What about cleaning? Do you have a crew that comes in? I don't imagine your nurses empty the waste baskets and clean up every night before they leave."

"I didn't think of them," Caden said. "But we've had the same cleaning service since shortly after I opened my practice. We've never had any trouble with them, but—"

"How long have you used them?"

"Two … No, now close to three years." Could someone on the two-person crew be behind the false narcotics prescriptions? He'd thought only of medical personnel as being able to send the prescriptions, but was that really true? All a non-medical person needed to prepare a legitimate-appearing prescription was a bit of training.

"What are you thinking?" Caruso asked.

Caden shook his head. "I was thinking that maybe our search has been too narrow."

"I don't understand."

Beth spoke up. "I think you also need to consider the DEA agents who've been conducting an investigation centered around this office. All we have is their word about why they're here. Maybe there's something else going on."

Beth looked at the clock in her kitchen. It was five in the evening on the longest day of her life. The picnic basket she and Caden had packed sat empty in the back seat of their car, forgotten as they dealt with the fire and its aftermath.

She could hear him in the front room, talking to the insurance company. "I'm telling you, this fire was deliberately set. Both the fire department and police told me that. I'm not going to argue with you about responsibility and coverage. Just tell me there'll be an adjuster at our office first thing Monday morning to talk about repairing the damage."

Several minutes later, he walked into the kitchen, muttering.

"Any luck with the insurance company?"

"It's a different company from the one that handles my auto insurance, and I don't deal with a local agent," Caden said. "That's something I'm going to remedy when it comes time for renewal. I finally got the person I talked with to promise to send an adjustor on Monday, although not necessarily first thing. I'll talk with the adjustor when they show, but something tells me it may be a slow process getting the fire damage repaired."

"Can we pay for things and then be reimbursed?"

"We could if we have to, I guess. I'll see." He walked over and hugged her. "I'm so very sorry you got involved in all this."

"We never know what's coming next when we marry someone," she said. "That's what 'For better or for worse' really means. And just to be certain there's no misunderstanding, I knew what I was doing when I recited those vows." She kissed him lightly.

They stood together in the center of the kitchen for a full minute before he said, "I guess there's nothing more I can do tonight. Do you want to go out for some supper?"

"Not really. How about something light?"

"Sounds great," Caden said. "Want me to help?"

Beth smiled. "Why don't you sit down at the kitchen table and talk with me while I get this together? That would keep you out of my way and speed up the process significantly."

When Caden's cell phone rang, he pulled it from his pocket, looked at the caller ID, and said, "I think this is Neilson's number."

When he started to get up, Beth said, "No. I deserve to hear this conversation. Put it on speaker."

Caden nodded. He answered the call and immediately punched the speakerphone button.

"What happened at your office? I drove by earlier today and saw a fire truck leaving. And there was a police cruiser out front."

Caden outlined what had happened. Then he said, "Since everyone thinks this was arson, a detective is involved. And I've already told him about your investigation and some of the fallout, including someone trying to shoot me."

"I thought we agreed to keep the local police out of this."

"No," Caden said. "You intimated that you wanted your investigation kept hush-hush, but I never agreed to that. I was wrong to wait so long before consulting an attorney. Then I almost delayed too long before I asked his advice again. But he and I talked recently, and he agreed I needed someone else on my side—someone in law enforcement that I can trust."

"You can trust me," Neilson said.

"I'm not certain about that. So far, it's been all take and no give from you and Harwell. I need to know when you're going to start making arrests. And, for that matter, have you found out anything about the other agent?"

"I'm close to winding everything up. Just give me a few more days."

"You can take as long as you want, but if you haven't contacted Detective Caruso of the Freeman police by the end of the day on Monday, I'll tell all my staff what's been going on. I'll blow your cover, and any element of surprise you have will be gone."

Neilson was saying something when Caden ended the call. He looked at Beth and said, "I suppose you think I was wrong to say that."

She shook her head. "No, I think you've been wrong to let them use you up to this point. You should have called Mel Sewell a lot earlier and kept him in the picture."

Caden nodded. "I just hope I haven't waited too long."

On Sunday morning, Caden tried several times to roll over and go back to sleep, but each time his eyes snapped open again as though the lids were spring-loaded. Finally, he slipped out of bed and moved softly to the kitchen. For a change, he'd remembered to set the automatic brew feature, so there was a full pot of coffee waiting for him.

He poured a cup and sat at the kitchen table. The newspaper was probably on the front lawn, but he made no move to get it There was nothing in it he wanted to read. No, this morning he wanted to sit quietly, sip his coffee, and try to make sense of the puzzle pieces that were his life.

Caden hadn't gotten far with his thoughts before he heard the shuffle of house slippers outside the kitchen door. Beth, a robe over her gown, entered the room, poured a cup of coffee, and joined him at the table. "What with inflation and all, I guess I should say a nickel for your thoughts."

"They're not worth even the original penny," he said. "I was trying to think through everything that's happened to me ... to us."

She leaned toward him and squeezed his free hand. "But is there anything you can do by worrying?"

"I guess not."

Beth took a sip of coffee, then set the mug down carefully before speaking. "We have to wait on your dad's diagnosis. We have to wait for the police to check into the fire. We have to wait for the DEA to finish whatever they're doing. We can't do anything about any of it right now. Right?"

"That's about the size of it."

Without speaking, Beth left the table. She was back in a few moments with her Bible. "Let's see if I can find what I'm looking for." She sat down, opened the book to about its midpoint, then thumbed through the pages until she found what she wanted.

"I'll bet you have something I need to hear," Caden said.

"How's this for advice. It's from Psalm 37: *Rest in the Lord and wait patiently for Him.*"

"So, I'm just supposed to relax, and God will take care of everything?" Caden said.

"No. But after you've done everything you can do, you depend on God to do what He's promised. It's a pretty good partnership that way." She gave her husband a smile. "Now, let's have breakfast and then get ready for church."

As Caden and Beth entered the First Community Church, he said, "I'd better sit on the aisle in case I get a call."

Beth looked like she was about to say something, but let it go. Caden figured it was a small victory, but he'd take whatever he could get.

A number of the congregation had apparently heard about Nancy Taggart's death and stopped by to offer their condolences. One of them was talking when Beth looked toward the platform and said, "I think Dr. Pearson is about to start."

The lady left, and Caden whispered to Beth. "I never know what to say to these people."

"Just thank them for their prayers. I think they're sincere."

Caden joined his baritone with all the other voices as he sang the familiar hymns—hesitantly at first, then stronger. After the first song, Beth put down her own hymnal and took her husband's free hand. They shared a faint smile and finished the hymn that way.

The pastor started in a conversational tone. "In a congregation this large, there is always a dire event. It may be in the wings, happening now, or just past. The week just ended has been no exception, as was the week before that, and the week before that, and … You get the picture.

"I've heard some of you say that if your faith is strong enough, God will protect you from bad things happening. I stand before you, a man of the cloth, holder of several degrees, supposedly an expert in theology, and I tell you that's not true."

There were murmurs within the congregation. Dr. Pearson let them die down before he continued, this time in a voice so strong it seemed the microphone before him was unnecessary. "Actually, we're told that the Christian *will* face troubles. It's promised in the Scriptures. And there are times when the load we're given—whether physical or emotional—is just more than we think we can bear. God's promise is that He'll provide the strength we need at the time we need it. And He'll ultimately guide us through it."

Pearson paused and scanned the congregation. "There's a great sign I saw on a desk recently. 'In the end, it will be all right. If it's not all right, it's not the end.'"

Caden looked at Beth and an unspoken message passed between them. She was right. It was up to him to do all he could, and then trust God to do His part.

18

The schedule for Monday lay on Henry Taggart's desk. He'd looked at it twice, and nothing had changed. It was still blank. He took a deep breath before bellowing, "Jean!" He didn't use the intercom button on his phone. The situation called for yelling, and he accomplished this by calling his nurse in a loud voice. She worked for him, not the other way around, and when he said he wanted to see patients, there should be patients on the list.

In a moment, Jean stood in the doorway of his office. She smiled sweetly. "I suppose the yell was because you've seen your schedule."

"Such as it is." Henry's tone reeked of sarcasm. He held up the schedule and waved it. "This is supposed to be a sheet of paper printed with the names of patients I'm scheduled to see today, but it's blank." He struggled to control his temper, but with little success. "Would you care to comment?"

Without an invitation, Jean entered the office, closing the door behind her. She crossed to the two chairs on the other side of Henry's desk and seated herself in one. "You didn't tell anyone on Friday why you were out, but I finally managed to wangle the information out of you. We talked for a bit on Friday night, and you told me about your biopsy, but nothing was said about your working today."

Henry felt his righteous indignation slipping away. That used to happen with Nancy when she made a good point. "You didn't ask me."

Jean didn't raise her voice, which served to frustrate Henry even more. "I never had the chance. So, I took it upon myself to keep your schedule open. I thought it would be better than canceling the appointments if you needed to take more time away from the office."

"Well, you were wrong." Even as he spoke, the doctor knew she was right. Jean wasn't taking over his life. She was simply doing what any good nurse would do.

It wasn't as though he was trying to build up his practice and see as many people as possible. Matter of fact, he'd already realized he needed to start cutting back, even though it seemed to him he was working harder for less money. Well, everyone was, he guessed.

Henry wasn't very good at apologizing, but he figured that's what he needed to do. "Jean, I'm sorry. I'll be here today, and rather than sitting around worrying or feeling sorry for myself, I'd rather see some patients. If you have some people you can contact and move up their appointments, especially those for a second opinion, I'll see them today."

"Yes, sir," she said.

He wasn't sure if Jean's words were meant to be sarcastic but decided to let it slide. Henry figured he'd done enough complaining for one day.

❧

Caden was full of apologies as he dropped Beth off at the office early Monday morning before heading for the hospital in his rental car to see the patient he'd been asked to consult on. "I don't know who's behind all this, but the thought occurred to me that they might want to get to me through you. That's why I thought we should ride together."

"I understand," Beth said, one hand on the door handle.

"I'm considering the possibility of having a security guard meet you in this parking lot each morning to escort you inside."

"Don't be ridiculous," she said. "There are already people in the building, even this early. I doubt anything will happen, but if there's someone lying in wait, I can get help." She held up her iPhone with her free hand. "It's just a phone call away."

"I don't know if that's enough," Caden said. "What if he shoots at you in a drive-by or uses a rifle while staying at a distance. Maybe I should sit here and watch you enter the building."

"Totally unnecessary." Beth kissed him and opened the door of the car. "I'll see you after you're through at the hospital."

Caden kept his cell phone within reach on the car seat beside him as he drove to his destination but resisted the temptation to call Beth. Maybe he'd text her when he reached the hospital—make sure she was safely in the office. The next minute he discarded that idea. If she didn't answer immediately, he'd hurry back to the office, only to find that she was fine.

At the hospital, Caden became engrossed in the consultation his friend, internal medicine specialist Tony Barnett, had requested. After a thorough history and physical examination, Caden decided this didn't represent possible appendicitis, despite the patient's belly pain and borderline elevation of his white blood cell count.

"Tony, I don't think he has a surgical abdomen. I agree you're wise to continue your work-up for chronic inflammatory bowel disease. I'll have a look at him again tomorrow. Meanwhile, have them call me if his symptoms change."

"Will do," Barnett said. "And I have to agree ... this is probably a case of irritable bowel vs. early Crohn's disease. In either case, so long as it's not an acute surgical belly, I'll pursue the other diagnoses."

Caden dictated a consultation note and talked a bit more with the patient. Then he decided he had time to stop by the surgeon's lounge. He doubted that the coffee had gotten any better, and Beth undoubtedly would have a steaming cup of a much better brew waiting for him when he got to the office—oh, wait. He didn't think anything in the break room was damaged, but maybe he'd better check that the coffee maker was working. One more thing to add to his to-do list.

When he walked into the surgeon's lounge, he found it empty. Despite his past experience, Caden decided to try a half-cup of coffee. If no one showed up by the time he'd either finished or tossed it, he'd leave and pick up one in the food court on his way out.

He took a couple of sips and decided that perhaps this was a bit better than the usual offering brewed in the lounge's coffee maker. As he sat down, Ann strolled in, turned up her nose at the coffee pot, and took a seat on the sofa next to Caden. She sat closer than usual. Was she sending a signal?

"Doing a case this morning?" Caden asked.

Ann ran the fingers of her hand through her short blond hair and nodded. "Ulcer with perforation of the duodenum," she said, referring to the part of the small intestine just beyond the stomach. "He came in last night. I was able to close the hole endoscopically."

"Patient doing okay?"

"Yes, but before he's discharged I need to have a talk with him. He'd been having belly pain going through to his back, so he treated it by gobbling ibuprofen like they were jellybeans. And, of course, that worsened his pain and eventually led to the ulcer perforating."

"Didn't he realize—"

Ann shook her head. "I know what you're going to ask. It never crossed his mind he could have an ulcer. 'I'm too busy for one,' he said."

Caden sipped more coffee. Either he was getting used to it, or this batch wasn't so bad. Maybe the hospital had so many complaints they'd changed suppliers.

Ann scooted even closer to him. Now they were shoulder to shoulder—not like colleagues. More like two people in a relationship. Caden wondered how best to extricate himself from what he feared was coming.

"I want to thank you again for being there to listen to me after my aneurysm patient died. And I hope I didn't—"

Caden stood, too uncomfortable to remain sitting beside her. He headed to the coffee pot, putting some distance between them. "Don't worry about it, Ann. You needed comfort. I was the closest person you could lean on."

"Actually," she said, "You weren't just the closest person. You were the right person."

With that, Ann jumped to her feet and hurried out of the lounge. He ran their conversation through his head but couldn't decide what it meant. Was Ann making a play for him? Or was she trying to divert his attention? And in either case, why?

Beth found when she walked into the office that, although she was the newest employee, she was looked upon as the person to answer all the questions. After all, she was the wife of "the boss."

"What happened over the weekend?" asked Donna, the receptionist.

"There was a fire in the records room. Thank goodness we had switched over to electronic medical records, so only the charts that we haven't digitized were affected. And those were primarily the ones of patients that haven't been seen here since right after the practice opened."

"So, our current records aren't affected?" Mona, the other receptionist, rolled her chair closer.

"If you need a record, check your computer. It should be stored in the Cloud." Beth looked at the others to make certain they understood. "And in case any of you are wondering, there are safeguards in place to keep hackers from accessing that information." *Which is why it makes no sense that our older records were targeted.*

"What about the fire damage in that room? Is the computer still working?" Mona asked. "Dr. Russell will be in the office this afternoon."

"Dr. Sparling is in surgery all day, but he's got people coming in tomorrow," Gary said.

"The computer is working fine, so you'll be able to call up charts and send electronic prescriptions. Dr. Taggart will talk with our insurance adjustor today about getting the damage repaired."

"So, it will be business as usual," Mona said.

"What about the men who were here last week?" Gary asked.

"They're gone, I guess," Beth said. She hoped. *I wonder when they're going to wind up their investigation.*

Caden was halfway through his morning when Beth tapped on the examining room door. "There's a phone call for you, Dr. Taggart."

He looked up from examining the man who lay on the exam table. "Can you take a message?"

"I believe it's urgent."

Caden frowned. "I'll be there in a moment." He turned back to the man. "You can sit up, button your shirt and pants, and make yourself comfortable. I don't think this is anything serious. Let me take this call, and I'll be back to talk about it."

At his desk, Caden punched the blinking button. "Dr. Taggart."

"This is Agent Neilson. I wanted you to know I contacted Detective Caruso this morning. Harwell and I are meeting with him tomorrow afternoon to fill him in. He's agreed to keep this under his hat for a few more days."

"Good," Caden said.

"I've met your deadline to liaise with the police, and now I want to make sure you're not going to blow my cover."

"When and where is this meeting scheduled? I want to be there. And my attorney will probably want to come as well."

Neilson stammered for a moment. "I don't know—"

"Look. You guys walked into my office and took over. I lied to my staff to give you a cover story. Now you're about to wind down the investigation, but in the meantime, there have been attempts to kill me. I think I deserve to hear what you have to say. And I believe Mr. Sewell does, as well."

There was silence on the other end of the line for almost a full minute. Finally, the agent said, "Let me check with the detective. I'll call back later."

When Caden came out of his office, Beth was in the hall outside. "That sounded like Neilson. Is something up?"

"I think we're nearing the end of this." He paused with one hand on the knob of the exam room door. "At least, I hope we are."

Since he'd been on his own, Henry Taggart's morning meal generally consisted of an English muffin plus coffee or juice—at least as much of it as he could force down. On Tuesday morning, he couldn't even tolerate the muffin. He sat at his kitchen table with a half-cup of cold coffee in front of him, waiting for the phone to ring. This morning the hands on the clock seemed stuck in quicksand, moving so slowly he wondered if it might need a new battery.

He thought back to the times when he and Nancy took advantage of the rare days when he didn't have early morning surgery. They'd enjoy waffles and sausage together. Then they'd have a leisurely second cup of coffee before he had to leave for the office. On those days, time seemed to fly by. Now he was alone.

Surely the biopsy had been read by now. Henry had been practicing surgery long enough to know how long it took for the pathologist to review biopsy specimens after they were prepared. Once the dictated report was transcribed, the pathologist read and initialed each page to be certain there were no errors. Eventually the ordering doctor would receive the report. Total elapsed time: two or three days, but less if the pathologist felt what he found was important enough for a phone call.

Henry figured that, since he was a physician, the pathologist might pick up the phone and call Dr. Ross with his report—unless there was a problem. But what if there were a problem? Was that what was taking so long?

His mind conjured up all sorts of scenarios. How many times had a radiologist or a pathologist told him they needed more views or additional specimens to give a firm opinion? Plus, this was cancer, not a diagnosis to be given lightly. What if Dr. Ross had to repeat the endoscopy and biopsies? What if this turned out to be some rare type of tumor that would prove to be beyond the point of treatment? What if—

Henry's phone rang. Not his landline, but his cell phone. Only a handful of people had this number, and one of them was Bradley Ross. *Oh, please, let it be him.* "Dr. Taggart."

"Doctor, this is Brad Ross. I hope I'm not calling too early."

"No, I've been up for quite a while. I presume you have news for me."

"Well, it's not what I hoped for, although it's sort of what we expected," Ross said. "But now we can move forward and lick this thing."

He hadn't heard the dreaded word "cancer" yet, but Henry knew what Ross was saying. There was no "this is terrible." Instead, Ross was saying that they—as a team—would "move forward and lick this thing."

Ross continued. "I was hoping we'd get lucky and the biopsy would show a benign neuroendocrine tumor, but this one's an adenocarcinoma. It's definitely malignant."

"Well, now I know for certain."

"I'll send a note to your internist, of course. And I notice that you originally saw Dr. Gershwin about the tumor. Do you want a copy of the report to go to him as well?"

Henry knew the question Ross was really asking was, "Will he be in charge of your treatment?"

Gershwin's approach had been, "Yes, you have a potentially fatal disease. We'll confirm it, then make you as comfortable as possible." By contrast, the attitude Ross had shown was that he, in partnership with his patient, would "move forward and lick this thing." And that was what Henry decided to do.

"You can send him a copy of your report, but if you don't mind, Dr. Ross, I want you to direct my treatment."

"I'll be pleased to do so. As a surgeon, I'm sure you realize the first step is to operate. And the sooner the better."

"Let's talk about that," Henry said. "Because I have someone in mind to do the procedure."

19

Since Beth started working at the office, their dinners were sometimes catch-as-catch-can affairs, and Caden accepted the trade-off. Tuesday evening, with Beth seated across their kitchen table from him, he chewed on a cold sandwich.

Beth had made a salad for herself, but after a few bites she put down her fork. "I'm sorry you couldn't be included in the meeting today."

Caden shrugged his shoulders. He drank a bit of iced tea, then wiped his lips with a napkin. "When Caruso called today, he said that since this was still an active matter he didn't want me there. He assured me I wasn't a suspect, but I am a witness."

"And your attorney?"

"I called to tell him. He said he'd stay in touch with Caruso, but that was okay for now." Caden picked up his sandwich but didn't take a bite. "Caruso told me that Neilson showed up by himself. He said Harwell had something else to do. I guess he didn't want to tip his hand about that part of the investigation."

"Did you get any sense that the police know who was behind the gunshots…" She shook her head and didn't finish the sentence.

"The attempt to lure me to the farmhouse and shoot me? I don't know. Meanwhile, Neilson tells me they'll be out of here in another day or two, and we can get back to our normal routine."

Beth pushed her salad away. "Well, at least you came out pretty well with the insurance adjuster."

Caden chewed and swallowed another bite of sandwich and followed it with more iced tea. "That was a relief. He assured me yesterday we could get the painters and carpenters in as soon as the fire inspector was finished with his investigation, which was signed off this morning. And since there was no equipment damage, it shouldn't take long to get things back to normal."

"By the way, I had a thought when I was explaining this to the staff yesterday morning. If our records are mainly electronic—"

Caden stopped her when their landline rang. He pushed back from the table. "Maybe it's my dad." He looked at the caller ID and nodded to Beth, who'd followed him into the living room.

"I'll pick up the extension in our bedroom," she whispered.

"Dad, it's good to hear from you," Caden said.

"Is this a good time?"

"Of course."

There was a click, followed by Beth's voice. "And I'm on the extension, so you have both of us."

"Any news, Dad?" Caden asked.

"I had the biopsy last Friday. Dr. Ross called me earlier today with the results. He found about what we expected—adenocarcinoma of the pancreas. I'd hoped it might be something other than that, but it's not."

Caden had trained at Parkland Hospital, and the UT Southwestern Medical Center had some of the best doctors around. But he wasn't certain he should mention the name he had in mind of the doctor his father should consult. Not yet. "So, what are you going to do?"

"I see Dr. Ross in a couple of days to plan this out, but you and I both know the first step is surgery to remove the cancerous mass. This is still a small tumor. There's a chance that a good surgeon can get it out intact. If it hasn't invaded blood vessels or spread to nearby structures, surgical resection gives me the best chance. Then we use chemotherapy and radiation to follow up."

Caden couldn't see Beth, but he could visualize her. She'd have her head bowed, her eyes closed, no doubt praying at that moment for his dad. *Include me, sweetheart, because I know what's coming.*

Sure enough, his father's next words were what Caden expected—and feared. "I want you to do the operation."

Caden had heard the expression "mixed emotions," but he'd never experienced it quite so vividly as now. "Dad, I'm glad to hear you talk about doing what's needed to beat this. But do you really think I'm the person to do the next stage—the surgery?"

"I know. Surgeons aren't supposed to operate on family and friends. Their judgment is affected by the relationship, and the surgeon has to be able to assess things unemotionally."

Caden found himself nodding, although he knew his father couldn't see him. "What if I got in and found the tumor to be beyond resection? What if the surgery was technically beyond my capabilities? Or what if I made a mistake? What if—"

"I know all the arguments. I've used them myself. Remember when you were in your early teens? You and Scott McElroy were scuffling, and you hit the table edge. I could have sewed up that laceration, but instead I got hold of the best plastic surgeon I knew."

Caden ran a finger over his left cheek. The scar had long since become almost invisible. He hadn't thought about that incident in years, but now that his dad mentioned it, the major emotion he remembered was fear. He wanted his father to sew up the cut. The man who eventually did it was a stranger to him. When the emergency room nurse tried to place a draping sheet around the wound, he'd cried out for his father. He didn't stop until he felt a hand grab his, and he held onto his dad throughout the entire procedure. "I understand."

"Will you do it? I can arrange temporary operating privileges at the hospital where my gastroenterologist works. One of the surgeons there can assist. He'll even do the post-op care. But I want you to do the case."

That evening, when Dr. Claude Horner arrived home, his wife was talking on the phone. He waited patiently for her to finish, although what he really wanted to do was snatch the instrument from her and share his news. While he waited, he went into the kitchen, opened the refrigerator, and treated himself to one of the two bottles of beer almost hidden in the back. He rarely indulged, but today was special.

His wife found him there, sitting at the kitchen table and gazing at the corner of the room. The bottle in his hand was half-empty.

"Sorry, that was my sister on the phone, and you know how she can talk."

Claude patted the chair next to him, and Nelda sat down. "I was at the hospital this afternoon and saw Jim Ketchersid as we were both walking out."

"Do I know him?"

"Not sure. He's a pathologist. He reads biopsy samples from all over town, and he told me he was sorry to hear about my partner."

Nelda's eyebrows went up. "Henry?"

"Yes. Jim had read the specimens Dr. Ross sent over... biopsy specimens from Henry." Claude drank deeply, emptying the bottle. "Adenocarcinoma of the pancreas."

"You've suspected that all along."

"Yes, but now it's confirmed. And that means there's an extremely good chance that Henry won't be around much longer. In turn, that means I'll be collecting the proceeds of his life insurance policy and can replace the money I've taken from the practice."

"But it's not a sure thing, is it?"

"The diagnosis—yes. The survival—it's only a matter of time."

Nelda frowned. "But the presence of pancreatic cancer isn't a 100 percent death sentence, right?"

"No, but time is on my side. This is going to happen."

The next day, Beth realized something was bothering Caden. He never shortchanged his patients, but between cases he seemed distracted. She was pretty sure what was occupying his attention, but it wasn't until lunchtime she had a chance to talk with him about it.

"Want to go out together and grab a bite?" she asked.

"I'm not hungry. Why don't you go with the other staff?"

"Bring you back something?"

"No ... Well, maybe a sandwich. I'll nibble on it if I get hungry later this afternoon. I want to spend some time at my desk, checking things on the computer."

"Why?" Beth asked.

"Because I need to call Dad this evening, and I want to be able to talk with him intelligently. The only way to get him to go along with my plan is to have the facts at my fingertips."

Seeing Beth's puzzled expression, Caden continued. "I called Dr. Ross about mid-morning. He and I agree that my old professor of surgery at the med center, Dr. Markham, is the best person to do the operation on Dad. He's done a lot of them, and this procedure should be handled by the person with the most experience. I've seen maybe three of these Whipple procedures, but I've never done one myself. Markham's performed at least fifty, maybe more."

"And you don't think your father knows that already?" Beth asked. "He's an experienced surgeon. He won't be unfamiliar with Markham's reputation. Surely he'll see that's the best man to do the procedure on him."

"You know how stubborn my father can be. Once he gets an idea in his head, sometimes you can't get it out."

Yes, as stubborn as his son ... the one who still harbors a suspicion that Jean had a hand in his mother's death.

Caden wasn't particularly anxious to get home on Wednesday evening and call his father, but he was ready for the day to be over. Unfortunately, as often happens in medicine (as in life), each time the end was in sight, something else came up. By the time he and Beth were finally ready to leave, the other two doctors, their nurses, and both receptionists had left.

At last, he joined Beth at the front desk after she checked out the last patient of the day. He looked with satisfaction at the empty waiting room. "Well, we did it."

"You mean you did it."

"No, I mean we did it," Caden responded. "I couldn't do it without you. I'll admit that I was disappointed when Rose said she had to leave and you insisted on stepping in, but you've done just fine as an office nurse."

"Thank you."

"And I think—"

Caden stopped when a young man dressed in a T-shirt, shorts, and jogging shoes came through the door of the office. His clothing was different from what most people wore for a visit to the doctor, but that wasn't the first thing Caden noticed. The man held a towel to his forehead, a towel that was gradually turning red. As Caden watched, drops of blood came through the cloth and fell on the waiting room carpet.

"I ... I'm sorry to come in here like this," the man managed to say. "I was jogging, and I fell. When I tried to get up, I ... I ..." He staggered and appeared about to lose his balance when Beth steered him toward one of the waiting room chairs.

"Don't worry about it," Caden said. "We'll get you taken care of."

"Can you walk back to the treatment room, or do you need a wheelchair?" Beth said.

The patient started to shake his head but stopped when blood ran down his face from the movement. "Just help me. I can walk."

Caden and Beth steered the man to a treatment room, where he managed first to sit and then to lie on the examining table.

"I'll have a look at the laceration on your temple," Caden said. "But first, let's make certain it's nothing more than that." He pulled on gloves and ran his fingers over the head wound. "What happened?"

"I stumbled while I was jogging in the next block. I started to fall, and I guess I hit the sidewalk, or maybe a rock."

"Were you knocked out?"

"I was stunned, but I don't think I lost consciousness."

"Where did you get the towel?" Beth asked.

"I had it tucked into the waistband of my shorts to wipe away sweat."

"Are you hurt anywhere else?" Caden asked.

"No. Just the cut on my head." The man tried to sit up but evidently decided that wasn't a good idea.

After checking the head wound and covering it with a bandage, Caden examined the patient for other injuries.

He concentrated on the neuro exam and was relieved by his findings. Finally, he straightened up from the exam table. "I think you're okay. You were stunned when you hit your head and sustained a large cut on your temple." He turned to Beth. "I'll need an X-ray of his skull to rule out any fractures. Then I'll put in some sutures on that wound."

"I'll make sure the radiology facility down the hall is still open," Beth said, and hurried from the room.

It took a while, but eventually, Caden put the last of six sutures into the man's head wound. Then Beth covered the laceration with a gauze bandage.

"Do you understand the concussion warnings we went over?" Caden said.

The patient nodded gently. "Wow, I didn't think moving my head would cause the trip-hammer behind my eyes to start up."

"And you'll need to see me or another doctor in about ten days for removal of those stitches. Do you have your own doctor?"

"Yeah. We're leaving town tomorrow, but I'll follow up with him." The man sat up slowly and made it this time. "I'll call my wife to pick me up." He reached for his hip pocket, then drew back an empty hand when he realized he was wearing running shorts. "May I use your phone? We're at the motel just a few blocks away."

Beth directed him to the phone. When his call was over, the man said, "I'm sorry, but I don't have any money or my insurance card or anything. I should have asked my wife to bring my wallet. Can I handle this later?"

Caden opened his mouth, but Beth beat him to it. She was getting to be an expert in this sort of thing. "Certainly. Let me get your name and address, as well as that of your doctor." She handed him a card with the office number on it. "The answering service will pick up any call to us tonight. Be certain to contact us if there's any problem."

It was late before Caden and Beth locked the door of the suite and walked out. As he opened the car door for her, he said, "I hope it's not too late to call Dad."

"Do you think you can put it off until tomorrow?"

Caden waited until he had seated himself and fastened his seat belt before he answered. "I'd love to put it off indefinitely, but I don't think I'd better. I just hope Dad will agree to see Dr. Markham about the surgery." He started the car. "I don't know how I'd get through doing his operation if he insists I do it."

That evening, Henry Taggart heard the "ding" of the microwave, but didn't rush to get up from his seat at the kitchen table. His evening meal was heated, but he'd long since ceased to look forward to TV dinners. He ate because he had to, not because he wanted to.

He had forgotten how unappetizing some of these "nuked" meals could be. They, and much of his loneliness, had gone away when Jean took on a larger role in his life than just an office nurse. But that changed when Nancy died. That was when Henry decided it was best to decline Jean's offers to cook for him, either at her home or his. She suggested once they meet at a restaurant, but he declined. He had likewise refused to let her come over just to talk. It didn't seem right any more.

Of course, they still interacted at the office, but in their last conversation Jean had said something that he didn't like to hear—from her or anyone. "Henry, you have some good years left, but only if you do something about it. You need to fight your cancer. Otherwise, it will kill you. You can't let that happen."

Under normal circumstances, Henry might let his relationship with Jean move forward after an appropriate time passed. After all, they'd known each other for a few years, and they were both single now. There was nothing wrong with his eventually marrying again. And Nancy would approve of Jean. Of course, Caden might not, but that was a bridge to cross sometime in the future. Right now, Henry realized he couldn't ask Jean to link her life to a man whose days were numbered.

So, here he was—back to eating microwaved frozen dinners alone. Maybe after his surgery, perhaps after he'd started chemo, he might resume his relationship with Jean if his prognosis somehow improved—but not now.

The microwave sounded again. Henry knew it would continue to do so until he finally opened the door and removed the TV dinner he was heating up. He'd always thought the second "ding" of the microwave was like someone saying, "Look, you were in a hurry, or you wouldn't have put whatever it is in here. Now it's ready. Come and get it, or I'll keep reminding you until you do."

As he rose slowly from his chair and made his way to the microwave, he wondered if the same didn't hold true of Jean's repeated offers to walk beside him through the next phase of his treatment. At this point, she wasn't offering to be his wife. She was offering to be what he needed most—a friend. He figured that eventually the microwave ding would stop … and so would Jean's offers.

Henry used a potholder to remove the food from the microwave and transfer it to the table. He took a fork from the drawer, grabbed a soft drink from the refrigerator, and sat down to eat. It was only then that he realized he didn't know what he'd heated up. Oh, well. It didn't matter.

After Nancy's death, after biopsy confirmation of his malignancy, he had given more thought to his relationship with God. He admitted in his heart that it had been tenuous for many years. He was trying to change that. Matter of fact, he'd made an appointment to talk with the pastor of the First Congregational Church. Maybe he'd even plan his own memorial service while he was at it.

Whatever the reason, he'd started saying a brief grace before tackling the unappetizing food before him. His typical prayer was, "Thank you for this food. I'm grateful that I'm alive to eat it. Amen." It wasn't much, but he figured that God knew what was in his heart.

He ate without thinking, almost mechanically. Then he cleaned the kitchen, although eating a microwaved meal directly from the package didn't leave much for him to do. He rinsed his fork and glass, put them in the dishwasher, and he was done.

Henry moved to his study, the room where he seemed to spend most of his time nowadays. As he settled into his recliner, the phone nearby, he tried to recall the quotation he'd read years ago, one attributed to a French military surgeon. It was something like, "I dressed the wounds. God healed the patient." Perhaps he needed to adopt that attitude about his own treatment. He had a good team of doctors. But he had to admit there was something missing—and it was up to him to remedy that.

Caden pushed back from the supper table. "I probably shouldn't put it off any longer. I think I'd better call my dad."

"I know all I had time to put together was just sandwiches and chips, but I thought you'd eat more than that." Beth started clearing the dishes from the table. "Is the call to your father bothering you that much?"

"Yes. It shouldn't, I suppose. I have no idea how my dad will react to my suggestion that the most experienced surgeon possible do his operation. I hope he'll look at the positive aspect of this, and not argue with me when I say I shouldn't be the one wielding the knife."

Beth eased into the chair next to Caden at the kitchen table and patted his hand. "You're doing the right thing. I know you—you're feeling guilty because you won't be the one operating on your father, but you know how wrong that would be."

Caden's expression reflected his mixed emotions. "I know."

"Tell him you'll be with him in the pre-op area, you'll be in the operating room, and yours will be one of the first faces he sees when he wakes up in the recovery room."

"And what am I supposed to do during the operation?"

"You know what to do," Beth said. "It's the same thing I'll be doing."

Caden took a deep breath, pulled out his cell phone, and speed-dialed his father. He could feel the perspiration begin to accumulate in his armpits, running down his side as the phone rang. "Dad, how are you?"

"Hanging in there," Henry said.

"Today I talked again with Dr. Ross. He's contacted Dr. Markham at the medical center, who has agreed to see you. If he thinks you have a surgically amenable lesion in your pancreas, he'll do the operation."

"But—"

He didn't want to give his father the chance to argue, so Caden plowed ahead. "Dad, he's the authority on this procedure. We could go anywhere in the country and not find anyone better qualified to do it. You know I shouldn't be the one doing this operation. But I'll be with you every step of the way—pre-op, surgery, recovery room. I won't leave your side."

In the silence that followed, Caden could hear his father breathing into the phone, so the connection was still open. *Please let him say yes.*

"I've been thinking about that," his dad said. That was followed by several seconds of silence. Finally, the answer Caden had been hoping for came. "You're probably right. I'll call and set up the appointment with him. I suppose he'll want to see the studies we've done so far, so I'll talk with his secretary about getting those."

The relief Caden felt lasted for only a few seconds. He wasn't going to be the surgeon performing his father's operation, but his role as a son was far from over. There was still a lot more to come.

20

On Saturday morning, Henry Taggart sipped coffee from a thick mug and let his mind run free. He was sitting in his favorite chair in the room Nancy used to call his "study." He guessed that's what it was, although lately it had been given over more to contemplation than to reading. He hadn't opened the journals and medical textbooks on the shelves behind him since he'd first been told he most likely had carcinoma of the pancreas.

He hadn't consulted a textbook or journal because there was no need for him to reconfirm what he'd known since his days in training. Oh, modern techniques had led to earlier diagnosis and better treatment, but the outlook was still dismal for patients. Such a diagnosis usually meant the patient had anywhere from a few months to, at best, a few years to live. Of course, there were exceptions, but they were rare. Doctors know that five-year survival statistics are a good indicator for longevity after treatment. But some patients believe they'll be on the far end of the bell curve—the end that beats the odds. Henry was more pessimistic. Or perhaps he was simply realistic.

When he'd called Dr. Markham's office at the medical center yesterday, the woman who answered the phone had been both helpful and considerate. She'd walked him through everything necessary to set up his appointment for Monday.

So now all he had to do was wait. That should have been easy, but he was finding it the hardest part of the process. Should he call Caden? No, he wanted to wait until his visit with Dr. Markham. There'd be plenty of time after that to talk with his son.

As he sat there, ignoring the coffee cooling in the mug he held, Henry realized that, although he was used to overseeing whatever situation occurred, in this case he wasn't. He wasn't Dr. Taggart, the surgeon, the doctor in charge. He was just plain Henry Taggart. He had cancer—a really bad form of cancer. And he was frightened.

Why had he pushed Jean aside when this was when he needed her most? He wasn't sure why. The reasons that seemed so valid recently didn't seem to hold water, not right now.

He wondered why she'd been so ready to walk beside him each step of the way to his diagnosis. Was it for his companionship? Henry realized he could be short-tempered, although he'd tried to change that. Did she want to marry him ... perhaps for the status it would provide, for the money that would be hers? No, there was no way he could believe she had that ulterior motive.

He shook his head as though there was someone in the room with him. Jean would never do that. He thought the woman had feelings for him, and just wanted to help—if in no other way, then by the simple gift of her presence in his life. And he was sorry he'd stopped accepting the gift.

The bottom line was that Henry Taggart was alone and frightened. He pulled out his phone, dialed a familiar number, and when the call was answered, said, "Jean? This is Henry. Can we talk?"

"Certainly."

She wasn't going to make this easy. Then again, he'd rebuffed her and probably hurt her the last time they'd talked. Their conversations at work had been professional but cool. He knew he needed to fix that. And he should do it face to face.

"Could you come over … please?"

Beth watched as Caden put down his phone, a disgusted look on his face. "No answer."

She shoved aside the knitting she was trying without much success to learn and turned in her chair toward her husband. "And that's the only number you have for Agent Neilson?"

Caden took a seat beside her on the living room sofa. "As I understand it, that's his cell phone number. But he's not answering."

"What else can you do?"

"I could do what my attorney did when I first consulted him. I could call the Seattle DEA office, but I doubt I'd get an answer on Saturday. I guess I could go looking for him, but I don't even know where Neilson and Harwell are staying. I'm stumped."

Beth took Caden's hand and patted it. "Are going through with what you threatened when Neilson called earlier in the week? Do you plan to tell the staff what the two men were actually doing in the office?"

"That threat sounded good when I made it to Neilson, but I've thought about it since then. If I let the staff know the DEA agents are investigating, whoever's responsible could just stop." He slowly shook his head. "I want this thing to be over because the people behind it have been arrested, not that they've just decided to quit for a while."

"I'm glad you got the local police involved. Maybe Detective Caruso can roll up this ring," Beth said. "Either with the DEA agents, or working on his own."

"I'm kicking myself for being so scared when the two men showed up at my office. I should never have cooperated with them without thinking about it. If I'd simply called their home office ... If I'd consulted Mel Sewell ... If, if, if."

"Stop worrying about it," she said. "This is all going to work out. Just be careful and trust in God. He has your back in all this."

"I'm glad someone does." He didn't say more, because at that moment his phone rang. "Maybe that's Neilson or Caruso."

From what she could hear of the conversation, Beth didn't think that was the case.

"I'll be right there," Caden said. He stood. "Ann has an emergency case at the hospital and needs my help in surgery. If I'm through by lunchtime, maybe we can finish that picnic lunch that was interrupted the other day."

As the patient was wheeled out of the operating room at a quarter to twelve, Caden snapped off his surgeon's gloves and flipped them into the waste container. His disposable mask and head covering went next. Then he stretched, trying without much success to relieve the tension built up in muscles that were tight after three hours spent at the operating table.

The incident that made the operation necessary started with heated words between the patient, Elvis Johnson, and another man inside a questionable club that should have been closed by that hour. The dispute eventually moved to the parking lot outside, where it ended with three gunshots to the abdomen of the unfortunate Elvis.

According to the police, no one knew the identity of the shooter, who had fled by the time they reached the scene. EMTs rushed Elvis to the ER at Freeman General Hospital, where Dr. Ann Russell examined him. She immediately arranged to do a surgical exploration of his abdomen—which is where Caden came in.

An orderly was cleaning up the OR and Caden was still stretching his back when Ann reentered the room. "Well, as I expected, there's no family in the waiting room. The nursing supervisor says they don't have an emergency contact or any information on the man beyond what they got off his driver's license."

"I guess we'll know more when he wakes up from surgery," Caden said.

"Or the police will find out. I appreciate your coming out to help me on a Saturday morning. But I'm afraid there won't be a fee for either of us in this one."

"I honestly don't know why you needed me for the case, but I was glad to help," Caden said. "I agree this was one we both probably did *pro bono*, but this is the sort of thing doctors sometimes do. A wise woman once told me that we all choose the brand of misery that makes us happiest. This is the brand of misery I've chosen."

Ann laughed. She looked up at the clock on the wall. "It's almost noon. The least I can do is buy you a late lunch. Give me a few minutes to change, and you can choose the restaurant."

Caden furrowed his brow. "I plan to call Beth, and if she doesn't have something else going on, I'd like to go home to her ... but thanks for the offer."

He was surprised by the expression that passed briefly across Ann's face after he said this. To Caden, it seemed to be like the expression on the face of a comic book villain when the balloon over his head says, "Curses, foiled again."

"Well, thanks for coming in to help me. I'll return the favor someday." Ann said. Then Ann turned on her heel and left the OR.

"Excuse me, doctor," the orderly said. "Can you move? I need to mop where you're standing."

"Sure. Sorry."

Caden exited the room, still trying to figure out Ann's reaction to his turning down her invitation in favor of time spent with Beth. If Caden had been the doctor on call, he figured he'd have inserted a self-retaining retractor and enlisted the help of a competent scrub nurse to assist him. Why did Ann think she needed his help? Surely, she hadn't asked for his assistance just so the two of them could have lunch together—had she?

Beth and Caden enjoyed a late lunch together, and now, the dishes cleared, they sat at their kitchen table enjoying the last of their iced tea. After a silence that seemed to last longer than usual, Beth looked at her husband. "You haven't said much since you got back from the hospital. Was it a tough case?"

Caden picked up his tea glass, then set it down without drinking. He kept his eyes away from Beth when he answered. "Multiple bullet wounds of the abdomen, but I think he'll make it."

"So that's good, isn't it?" Beth suspected there was something more on her husband's mind. He didn't say anything further, but she knew it would eventually come out.

"I don't know what to make of Ann Russell."

Beth moved her chair closer to Caden and took his hand. "What do you mean?"

She listened as he related the way Ann had acted after the last couple of cases in which he'd assisted.

Caden looked up at her. "I know this sounds conceited…"

"What?"

"It's almost as though she's decided that the only way she can have me is to take your place."

"I'm flattered," Beth said, "But don't you think there's another explanation?"

"You mean she's trying to distract me from paying attention to this DEA investigation?" Caden massaged his chin. "I've sort of discarded that theory. I mean, I've known Ann since residency. I'm pretty certain she's doing well financially, so why would she jeopardize that by adding an illegal activity."

"How well do you really know her?" Beth asked. "Yes, you were in residency together. She said she was coming here at the same time you did because she wanted to get away from a failed engagement. But did you ever see an engagement ring? Did you meet this almost-fiancé?"

Caden shook his head.

"You make a comfortable living, and we live simply. As I recall, Ann has a house all to herself in a nicer part of town. She drives a nicer car. She's gone on a couple of cruises. Where does she get that money?"

"I don't know. Then again, I thought I saw something between her and Harwell the first time the DEA agents met the other doctors in my office. I guess she could be involved in this investigation."

Henry Taggart opened his front door and stepped back. "Jean, come in. Thank you for coming."

"I'm happy to come over any time," she said. "But the last time we talked I got the distinct impression that perhaps you didn't want to see me for a while."

"Not at all," he said. "I just needed to think things over. Besides, I thought you'd probably appreciate some time to yourself."

"Well, I've certainly had that."

Henry didn't know how to interpret that remark. Was she angry? He hoped not. "Let's go into the living room and talk." He ushered her in and pointed toward the sofa. She took a seat, and he sat next to her. Where should he begin?

It didn't appear Jean was going to help. She crossed her legs and leaned back. "As they say in the business world, you called this meeting."

He'd thought this through. Now if he could only remember how he wanted to say it. "When your husband was killed in that car accident, Nancy offered her support, but I'd like to think I was there for you too."

"You were," Jean said.

"And then, starting at the time of Nancy's stroke, all during her time in the nursing home, even when she died, you've been there for me to lean on."

"That's what friends do."

"But it seemed to me you went beyond that. When my diagnosis of pancreatic cancer first came up, you were the one I turned to for support. If Nancy had been alive, she would have been there for me. But that was impossible, so you stepped in and did what my wife would have. You were there for me at every turn, and it helped. It was important to have someone to talk with, someone to tell me things would be okay."

"I was simply there with what you needed," Jean said.

"I know you thought you were acting as a friend," Henry said. "But recently it's become pretty clear you're more than a friend to me. I've developed feelings for you. I shoved those aside while Nancy was alive, but now she's gone."

Jean looked at him but remained silent.

Henry wiped his palms on his trousers. "In a few days, I'll undergo radical surgery. After that will come radiation or chemo, maybe both. And there's only a small chance that treatment will stave off the inevitable end." He swallowed a couple of times, but the dryness in his throat wouldn't go away. *Here goes.* "Jean, I'm afraid to be alone for the journey."

"Caden is still here. So is Beth. And you have your friends."

"My son and daughter-in-law are wonderful, but they have their own lives," Henry said. "And as for friends ... they were mainly Nancy's. I know now that I've spent too much time with my practice and not enough with the people who cared for me."

"It's not too late to change that," Jean said.

"I hope not, and I plan to start now." Henry drew a deep breath. "I know that my future is clouded at best and dim at worst. But over the past several weeks I've come to realize that I care for you—more than just as a friend. And I think you care for me." He paused, like a man at the edge of a high diving board. "Jean, I love you. I want you to be a part of my life … whatever's left of it."

Jean's lips moved, but no words came out of her mouth.

He'd hoped she'd say it back to him, but she hadn't … yet. Once he'd spoken the "L" word there was no turning back. Henry hurried on before he lost his nerve. "Jean, I have a tough road ahead of me, but I've made up my mind to fight the cancer all the way. And I want you by my side." He took a deep breath. "Will you marry me?"

21

Caden sat next to Beth in their usual location at the back of the sanctuary of Freeman's First Community Church. All around them, people were talking to the folks next to them, some stood in the aisles and visited, but Caden didn't feel like interacting with anyone. He sat with his head bowed, not so much in prayer as in hopes that no one would bother him.

As he continued to sit there quietly, an island of silence in the midst of the crowd, his thoughts turned to the problems facing him—problems he'd finally decided he couldn't solve, couldn't even get through, without God's help. It was a shame that these events had brought him to his knees, but he recalled what President Lincoln was purported to have said. "I have been driven many times upon my knees by the overwhelming conviction that I had nowhere else to go."

"Care to share your thoughts?" Beth whispered as though she were hesitant to interrupt her husband's silence.

He raised his head and tried to manage a smile. "Just thinking about everything that's going on. It's been almost a month since the DEA agents appeared in my office. They promised to be gone soon, but they're still around, even though I can't contact them."

"That's—"

Caden continued. "My mother has died. I'm still not sure his nurse didn't have a hand in that, so she could marry Dad. And, of course, I've been locking horns with him to fight this diagnosis he's been given rather than giving up and ending his own life."

Beth looked around her before she spoke again. "You're not going to change any of that for the next hour or so. Why don't you lose yourself in the service? Maybe God will speak to you and give you strength and wisdom. Maybe not. But at least give Him a chance."

Henry Taggart lay in bed on Sunday evening—or, more properly, Monday morning. He didn't look at the clock on his bedside table. The last time he'd glanced that way, it showed 2:00 a.m., and he hadn't slept since that time—or before, for that matter. Then again, there was no need for him to know exactly how long he'd been in the grip of insomnia. The simple answer was "all night."

He had to admit that his proposal to Jean had been affected by his fear. He was afraid he'd die alone, with no one to comfort him, to hold his hand as he slipped from this life to the next . . . or to oblivion. True, there were Caden and Beth, but as he'd told Jean, they had a life of their own.

Oh, he knew all the reasons Jean might be cozying up to him. If she were his wife she'd have financial security, status as a doctor's wife, freedom from work. And he'd picked up on the signals his son exhibited, signals that Caden resented Jean, fearing she was trying to replace his mother.

But none of that stopped Henry from asking Jean to share what life he had left. He knew what lay ahead—he was a surgeon, after all—and he decided there was no way he could face it alone. But Jean's reaction surprised him.

"Henry, I'm flattered that you asked. Would it be terrible if I asked for a day or so to consider this?" She'd smiled. "I know it's trite, but 'This is so sudden' actually describes my feelings right now. I need to think about this—actually, I need to pray about it."

"Of course. I started to tell you to take all the time you need," he'd said. "But, considering that I need to get started in my battle against this cancer—don't take too long."

Well, you've done it, Henry. If she says yes, you'll have to tell Caden and Beth, which may not be pleasant. And if she says no . . . I don't even want to think about that. I have too many unknowns in my life already.

Henry fidgeted as he sat in the office of Dr. John Markham on Monday, waiting for the man to return. He had come to this appointment alone, but he already wished he'd called Jean and asked her to accompany him. Not because this visit with Dr. Markham was so terrible. He liked the consultant, and thus far he'd gotten along well with him. Yet he thought that Jean's presence would make the visit even more tolerable. But he and Jean were in a no-man's-land right now about their relationship. And that made him long for her reassuring presence even more. It really did help to have someone to lean on for comfort.

Henry's idea of a surgeon at the medical center—any faculty member for that matter—was an individual who was aloof and cold. But that wasn't the case here. Markham was warm, understanding, and collegial. He'd treated him as an equal, pointing out technical details on the studies and talking about what he'd need to do to perform successful surgery. It was as though they shared a common goal—and, come to think of it, they did.

Markham walked in and closed the office door, putting an end to Henry's daydreams. "Sorry to keep you waiting. I had to talk with one of the residents about a case."

"No problem," Henry said, although his time waiting had increased his anxiety level until he felt he was about to jump out of his skin. He went right to the question that was foremost in his mind. "Do you think I'm an appropriate candidate for a Whipple?"

"Yes," Markham said. "Usually, pancreatic cancer is diagnosed late—too late for us to do more than palliation. Yours is early. I know you're a surgeon, but I'll ask what I ask of all, my pre-op patients. Do you understand what's involved in the surgery? How extensive it is? The risks and consequences?"

Henry said he did, but still Markham extracted a ballpoint pen from his white coat and used a pad to show exactly what he planned to do. Then he listed the possible complications. "Knowing all this, are you still willing for me to perform the surgery?"

"Yes."

Markham smiled. "It's amazing how often people decide not to proceed with surgery when I start detailing the possible complications and the hoped-for results. But I think it's best to get it all out in the open now rather than having them back out once we've scheduled the procedure."

Henry decided that now was the time to ask the other question he had. "My son is a surgeon—trained here, matter of fact. And it would be a tremendous favor if Caden could be with me in the pre-op area and in the recovery room."

"We may be able to arrange that," Markham said. "I think I remember Caden. Good surgeon. I'll be glad to see him again."

"Would it be possible for him to be in the OR during the procedure?"

Markham screwed up his face. "Since he doesn't have privileges here, the usual answer would be no. But let me talk with the department chairman, maybe the president." He held up a finger as though emphasizing his point. "If we make the exception, though, he'll have to stand back and be quiet. There'll only be one surgeon in charge of this case. It's not a matter of ego. It's just the way things should be."

"I appreciate your checking, and I'm sure Caden will abide by your wishes," Henry said. "Now when can you do the operation?"

"I've got everything cleaned up. Last night I took care of the last person involved in what we do. The only people left are you and me. Now it's time to execute the final stage."

"Are you certain there's no other option besides what you call Plan B?"

"Look. I'm in charge. This is the best way to wind things up. You just do your part. By tomorrow night, it'll all be over."

Beth was standing with Caden in the hall outside an exam room as he was about to see his first patient. "Today looks to be pretty quiet."

Before he could reply, one of the receptionists, Donna, hurried up and spoke to Caden. "Dr. Taggart, I just got a call from Dr. Russell. She seems to have come down with the flu and won't be in today. She's scheduled to see a couple of post-op patients and wondered if you'd take care of them for her."

"Sure. Beth, I can handle a couple more patients, can't I?"

She thought a minute. "Shouldn't be a problem."

Caden turned to Mona. "Just let the other receptionist know what's going on. How about surgical cases tomorrow? If Ann really has the flu, I doubt that that she will be well in one day."

"She has a couple of fairly straightforward elective cases in the morning, and Dr. Sparling said he'd do those if the patients agree. Gary is calling them now."

"Let me know if she calls again. I'd like to talk with her."

"I don't think she's going to want to talk much," Donna said. "Her voice was sort of a whisper when she called me. But I'll let you know if she phones."

Mona started to leave, then turned back. "Dr. Taggart, I guess this is none of my business, but something seems a little off about all this."

"What's that?"

"When I told Gary about Dr. Russell's call, he got the strangest look on his face. Nothing specific—just an expression like you'd get if you thought something was wrong."

Caden looked at Beth, who shrugged. "Thanks for telling me. I'll keep an eye on things."

When Caden stopped for a breather mid-morning, Beth followed him into his office and sat down. She handed him a Diet Dr Pepper and opened the one she'd brought for herself. "Any word from Ann?" she asked.

"No. I thought maybe I'd go over there at noon and see if I can do anything for her."

"Why don't I go with you?"

Caden took a sip from his cold drink and set the can aside, carefully placing a coaster under it and earning a nod from his wife for remembering. "I suppose so."

Beth grinned. "I know this might not have crossed your mind, but it's probably a good idea to have another female present when you see her."

"No, actually I'd already thought of that. Thanks for volunteering to go with me."

Henry waited until he was in his car in the parking lot of the medical center before pulling out his cell phone and dialing his son's office number. He wanted to accomplish two things—tell his son how his appointment with Dr. Markham went and make certain Caden agreed with the ground rules the surgeon had set up.

His call was forwarded to Beth, who said Caden would be finished with his patient shortly. Should she get him out of the room? Henry said it would keep. He asked that his son call his cell phone when he was free, then settled down to wait in the parking lot. He didn't want to be driving while talking with Caden. No, this was too important. It would demand all his attention.

Ten minutes, then fifteen passed with no return call, but Henry didn't worry. He had practiced surgery for well over two decades and knew how often five minutes turned into fifteen or twenty in a surgeon's life. He'd been waiting eighteen minutes when his cell phone rang with Caden's return call.

"Son," Henry said. "I saw Dr. Markham today. We went over my tests together and talked about the treatment options. He's willing to do the surgery in a week, and then turn the rest of my care over to Dr. Ross." He paused to swallow. "He thinks I've got a chance to beat this thing."

"Dad, that's great."

"I want you to be with me in the pre-op and post-op area, as well as during surgery if it's possible. Markham is checking."

"I'll be glad to do that," Caden said. "Did you like Dr. Markham?"

"My like or dislike isn't as important as whether I think he's a good surgeon, and I do. But, to answer your question, not only do I have no problem putting myself in his hands from a technical standpoint, but I like the guy. I think if we'd met under different circumstances, we might be friends."

"Don't rule that out even yet," Caden said. "My attitude is this is a problem you need to deal with before you get on with your life. After that, who knows?"

Henry wondered if he should tell his son that he'd asked Jean to marry him. He decided to postpone telling Caden and Beth until he heard the answer to that all-important question. Of course, if she said yes, then he'd need to deal with his son's theory that Jean was responsible for the death of his wife. He couldn't believe that was a serious consideration. For now, he'd move ahead one step at a time.

When Caden pulled his rental Camry up to the end of the circular drive in front of Ann's home in one of the nicer sections of Freeman, he looked at Beth in the seat beside him, and his lips formed a silent, "Wow."

"Exactly what I was thinking," Beth said. "I was trying to remember whether Ann has ever had us over. She's hosted dinner for us and the Sparlings at the country club, but never here."

"I never think of things like that," Caden said. "I work with Ann, see her professionally, but—"

"But you never think of things like social obligations. Well, women do. And I suspect Ann has hosted us at the country club because she doesn't want us to see her home."

Beth looked once more at the two-story home that she estimated at four thousand square feet or so, the perfectly manicured landscape that only a gardener could manage, and the large plot of land on which it all sat. "I wonder if Ann is hiding this place from all of us."

Caden opened the door of his Camry. "Well, we're here now. Let's go see how Ann is feeling."

He rang the doorbell but heard no stirring inside the house. Another push with no result. "Maybe the bell is broken." Caden knocked, and when there was no response, knocked even louder.

"Should we have called to let her know we were coming?" Beth asked.

"I didn't think about it." Caden pulled out his cell phone. "Perhaps I should—"

Footsteps inside the house made him put away his phone.

"Someone's coming. Maybe she was in bed. I know when I had the flu, I wanted to rest and not be bothered." Beth looked at her husband. "Maybe this wasn't a good idea."

"Those footsteps are heavier than Ann's. I wonder if she has someone here taking care of her."

The door opened, and a familiar voice said, "Come inside, you two. I wondered how I was going to lure you here, Dr. Taggart. Now, not only have you come right to me, but you brought your wife with you. How convenient."

Darren Neilson gestured with the pistol he held. "Inside. Now!"

22

Henry went to his bank, put gasoline in his car, and in general killed time rather than going where he knew he needed to. Finally, he could put it off no longer. He parked his car and walked into his office. He found Jean in the workroom, where she was cleaning instruments and putting them into sterile packs.

"I'd like you to go out to lunch with me," he said.

"Henry, I—"

"I don't want to make this an order, but I am your boss—as least for a bit longer. I went to Dr. Markham's office this morning, and I need to talk with you about what comes next." *Should he ask her for an answer here or wait?* After a pause that was probably too long, he said, "And I'd like an answer to the question I asked two days ago."

Jean nodded. She dried her hands on a paper towel, then looked at her watch. "Let me tell Dr. Horner's nurse that I'm leaving."

Henry waited nervously. He didn't know which was worrying him more—talking about what lay ahead with his surgery and the treatment to follow or getting the answer from Jean that would determine whether she'd be beside him during that time.

Beth hadn't been working at Caden's office when the agents initially showed up, nor had she met either of them later. However, her husband's first words identified the man holding the gun.

"Neilson, what are you doing here. Where's Ann? What's going on?"

"Ann is fine. She's in the bedroom packing. I think the work she and I started here is ready to be brought to an end."

"I don't understand," Caden said.

"Simple. She's been my partner in this from the beginning. It takes a while to set up, but it's been very lucrative. Using my position in the DEA, I've managed a number of these operations. She's the one who's been using the computer in your workroom to send those fake narcotics prescriptions. We figured just two a week wouldn't arouse too much suspicion. Most of the time we used your DEA number or Sparling's, but she mixed in her own a few times just to avoid suspicion."

"How did you pull it off?"

"We paid homeless alcoholics a hundred bucks a piece to pick up each prescription, using false names. We hired a dealer to repackage and sell the product. And we were still able to split almost a million dollars a year."

Beth spoke up for the first time. "But if things were going so well, why are you quitting?"

Neilson grinned, but there was no mirth behind his expression. "Because someone saw Ann sending a prescription a couple of times and got suspicious. And it unraveled from there."

Beth looked at Caden. *The anonymous phone calls warning him not to trust the DEA. Who made them?*

"At first, we thought it was no big deal," Neilson said. "Then he saw her several more times, and it became obvious he was watching her. After that, when she saw him going through the inactive files looking for the names of your old patients, we knew we had to do something. That's when I submitted an anonymous tip to the Seattle field office and got myself assigned to investigate."

"But—."

He waved the gun at the sofa. "Sit."

"What's your plan?" Caden asked.

"Hurry up," Neilson called over his shoulder. Then he turned back to Caden and Beth. "While I was here, I closed all the loopholes. That involved eliminating a number of the people we used to pick up the narcotics, as well as the dealer who was selling them for us." He waved his pistol to make it clear what that "elimination" involved.

"And now?"

"Now I shoot both of you, load you in the trunk of Ann's leased Cadillac, and leave it at the airport in long-term parking. She disappears and resurfaces in Nebraska, where she'll use another name to take and pass the tests to be licensed there. She'll get a DEA number—the story we plan to use is that she never got one because she's been overseas   and we start all over again."

"Surely someone will find our bodies," Beth said. When she realized what she'd said, she felt chills creeping down her spine.

Neilson shrugged. "Just another execution-style death linked to drug-dealing."

"Won't the police come after you when the real story comes out?"

"You don't get it, do you? We intend to pin all this on you, Dr. Taggart."

"You started the fire at the office?" Caden said.

"No." Ann Russell stood at the foot of the stairway, carrying two large pieces of luggage. "I did that. Burning a few of the inactive charts would make it impossible to prove the patients that went with those scripts didn't exist."

"So, you weren't watching Harwell?" Caden asked.

"Harwell was watching me," Neilson said. "I couldn't stop the office from sending him here too. But he won't be watching anymore. There's a large cistern behind that abandoned farmhouse you drove to. It was a good place to get rid of him. My report will say that Harwell disappeared about the time you and your wife did."

"Let's get this over with," Ann said. "I'm sorry to leave this home, but it's mortgaged to the hilt anyway, so it's not as though I'm walking away from something I can't replace in a few months." She dropped the heavy suitcases. "Why don't we let my colleague and his wife help me out to the car with these?"

Slowly, Beth and Caden moved toward Ann as Neilson followed them, his pistol still pointed in their direction. They were halfway to the suitcases when Beth heard a familiar voice.

"Stop right there, Neilson. Drop the gun and move toward Dr. Russell."

The voice bore the ring of authority. Gary, Dr. Sparling's nurse, stepped through the doorway, still wearing scrubs like all the other office nurses, but his demeanor had changed. Gary's finger was on the trigger of a revolver, and the way he held it signaled that he knew how to use it.

Ann stopped where she was, but Neilson—whether by instinct or prior training—whirled and fired. Caden saw this, and without thinking he launched himself at the agent in a flying tackle. He hit Neilson just as he fired a second time, which made the shot go over Gary's head.

Caden knew he had one chance to end this struggle, so he launched a vicious forearm strike, one that connected with the agent's chin. Neilson fell backward, the pistol still in his right hand. From the look of the man's limp posture and closed eyes, he was unconscious.

"Don't move, Dr. Russell." Gary's pistol was firmly pointed toward Ann. "Dr. Taggart, are you okay?"

"I'm fine. Just a bit overwhelmed."

"By what we've learned, or by your actions?" Beth asked.

"Both."

It was Monday and the noontime crowds were relatively thin, so Henry was able to get a table at the restaurant where he used to take Nancy. There were no other diners near enough to overhear their conversation. The mood and location were right. Now if he could just say it properly—and get the right response.

"What about your visit with Dr. Markham," Jean said as soon as they were seated, and their drink orders taken.

"I think I have two excellent doctors on my case," he said. "Dr. Markham and I spoke frankly about the Whipple procedure. He thinks we've caught this lesion early, and the surgery will most likely remove all the tumor. After I heal, Dr. Ross will take over. We'll discuss chemotherapy and/or radiation at that time." He spread his hands. "I've made up my mind to stop being a doctor and concentrate on my role as a good patient."

"How about Caden?"

"Assuming we can get the proper permissions, he'll be with me every step of the way—not as a surgeon, but as my son."

Conversation ceased as iced tea was served for both of them. They each glanced at the menus and ordered.

When the waiter left their table, Henry reached out for Jean's hand. He was encouraged when she slid it into his. "As I recall, I told you two days ago that I love you. That hasn't changed, and I don't think it will. I want you to be a part of my life…whatever's left of it. Now I'll ask you again. Will you marry me?"

Jean took a deep breath. "Henry, I love you too. I'm glad you've decided to fight your cancer, and I'll be by your side every step of the way. I'll even nurse you if you get too weak to help yourself."

"I sense a 'but' coming."

She left her hand in his. "But I'm not ready to marry you right now. It's not that I don't want to be your wife. I'd like that…someday. But it's too soon after Nancy's death. If you still want to marry me in a year, we can discuss it again."

He wanted to be able to lean on Jean, and she'd assured him that she'd be there for him. She simply didn't want to marry him this soon after Nancy's death. He could see that. His son had made it an open secret that he figured Jean would do everything she could to become his wife. But she'd been given the opportunity and declined for now, but not forever. She simply thought it was a decision best put on hold for a year.

"When the time comes for your surgery, I'll be there," Jean said. "Is there anything I can do in the interim?"

He continued to hold her hand. "As I've said, I believe I have the best doctors. Every one of them has said he's praying for me. Other than letting them do what they do best from a professional standpoint, it's in God's hands. So, I've joined them in praying. It's something I should have been doing for years. But better late than never, I guess."

"And I've been praying for you too," Jean said, "even when you didn't want me to."

He smiled. "I suspected as much."

It was still Monday, although late in the afternoon, and even though the squad room was a hive of activity, no one seemed to be paying attention to the group gathered around Detective Sam Caruso's desk.

Caden and Beth sat across the desk from the detective. Gary was seated to Caruso's right in a chair that he'd pulled over from another desk. He was still in his scrubs, but his pistol was no longer in evidence.

"Will the police take over from here?" Caden asked.

Caruso shook his head. "I imagine the DEA will send a team from the regional office to finish investigating the false prescription ring Neilson and Dr. Russell were running. The murder of a federal official such as Agent Harwell falls under the purview of the FBI, but the DEA will want to be in on that one. Holding you and Ms. Taggart at gunpoint is technically kidnapping, so again the FBI will be involved."

"What about luring me to that farmhouse and trying to shoot me?" Caden asked.

"Since that's outside the city limits, the county sheriff's office will investigate in conjunction with the FBI." Caruso leaned back in his swivel chair and put his hands behind his head. "It's going to be a mish-mash of law enforcement agencies, but you all needn't worry about it until it comes time for you to testify. Will that be a problem, doctor?"

"Not at all," Caden said. He looked over at Gary. "But how did you get involved in this?"

"As you may have figured, I was the anonymous voice on the phone. My cousin called me about the time the DEA agents showed up at our office. He's with the Seattle police department, and they'd been keeping an eye on Neilson because they thought he was bending the rules, maybe breaking a few. They just couldn't catch him. Since my cousin heard he was coming to Freeman, I made it a priority to watch him."

"And when you saw Dr. Russell using the computer to send out a prescription, what made you suspicious?" Beth asked.

"It's unusual for her not to tell her nurse to do that, but she certainly had the right to send it herself. Mainly, when I saw her do it, I was struck by the guilty look on her face. Then I saw that same look when I walked in on her several more times. It was the same look a kid displays when their mother catches them doing something forbidden. That's when I began to wonder if maybe she was up to something."

"But why did you show up at Dr. Russell's house? Not that I mind." Beth smiled at him.

Gary shrugged. "I overheard the conversation when Dr. Russell called to tell Mona she was home with the flu. Something didn't seem right. So, when you two went to go check on her, I decided to use my lunch hour to do some snooping. I followed you, parked a block away, and listened at the partially open front door. When I heard Neilson talking about what was going on, I decided to step in before you got hurt."

Detective Caruso looked at Gary. "By the way, we checked on your permit to have that weapon. It's all in order. You must have remembered a lot from those classes."

"That's why I have it," Gary said. "I usually leave it in my car when I go to work. However, I'm glad I had it when I confronted the man at Dr. Russell's house.

Early that evening, Henry sat down in his recliner and called his son. He'd been dreading telling him how Jean responded to the proposal. He hoped there wouldn't be a fight. But putting off the moment wouldn't make it any more unlikely.

"Is Beth there?" he said.

"She just walked into the room, Dad. Let me put this on speaker so you can talk with both of us."

Henry took a deep breath. *Here goes.* He described how Jean had responded to his proposal. The good news was that she had the same feelings for him that he'd developed over the past year. And she'd promised to be beside him every step of the way of his journey. But she felt it was too soon after Nancy's death for either of them to consider marriage.

"I suppose that makes you happy," Henry concluded.

"Not really, Dad. I'll admit that I've been harboring the suspicion that Jean wanted to become your wife, mainly because of the perks it carried. But since she turned you down, or at least deferred a positive answer to your proposal, I guess that shoots that theory. However, I'm glad she'll be there by your side through this journey."

Caden promised to make himself available for whatever role Dr. Markham would allow him and to pray for his father in the interim. Both pieces of news thrilled Henry. He hadn't been a very good model for Caden when it came to religion in general and praying specifically, but if God granted him the time, he planned to change that.

"Caden," Beth said. "You need to tell your father what happened to us this afternoon."

"I don't want to upset—"

Beth's voice became more forceful. "Caden, I think your father can take hearing about our situation. Besides, it's all over now."

"Okay. Dad, we had a bit of excitement this afternoon. Let me say that we're fine, and the whole thing is settled. I was still debating telling you about it, since you've got so much on your plate. But I guess you need to know."

Henry listened as Caden related how he and Beth were held at gunpoint, their rescue, and the underlying plot that had been revealed.

"But you're not in any danger now?"

"No, we're fine. We met with the Freeman detective who's handling the investigation. I suspect there'll be a number of law enforcement agencies involved before it's brought to a conclusion, but other than testifying, we're out of it."

During his son's relating of the events, Henry felt his heart beat speed up and the cold sweat form on his forehead. When Caden wound up his narrative, his dad said, "Thank God you and Beth are okay."

There was a brief pause before Caden's next words. "Are you serious about the thanking God? That just doesn't sound like my father."

"I know. It seems a bit out of character for me, but that's something I intend to change. I talked with the pastor, and he assures me it's never too late." Henry swallowed. "I hope he's right."

They talked for a bit more before Henry said, "I hate to cut this short, but Jean's coming over tonight. She volunteered to cook supper, and I decided that it would be foolish of me to turn down a nourishing, home-cooked meal when I should be building myself up for the surgical procedure next week."

Caden's chuckle came through clearly. "Sounds reasonable to me." There was a pause before he continued. "Dad, I'm happy you're letting God be a part of your life now. I'm trying to do the same thing. And I'm glad Jean is going to be with you through this. Give her my love."

Henry was still sitting in his recliner when the doorbell rang. He'd intended to give Jean a key but hadn't gotten around to it yet. He heaved himself out of the chair and went to the front door. Without looking, he opened the door and said, "Jean. Come in."

But it wasn't Jean on the front step. It was another woman, and she held a pistol aimed directly at his chest.

23

Nelda Horner stepped inside and kicked the door closed behind her, the pistol never wavering.

"Nelda, what's the meaning of this? Why the gun?"

"Anyone who knows anything realizes that carcinoma of the pancreas is a death sentence. I just don't know when your time will come. Claude was willing to wait, but I'm going to hasten it a bit." She gestured with the gun. "Your study should serve nicely. Of course, that's just a fancy word for the place you sit in your recliner and think."

"I don't—"

"You've told Claude about the study. I understand that after Nancy's stroke you spent a lot of time in there. That's probably where you first considered suicide. And I think it would be a good place to stage the end of your life." Again, she gestured with the gun, and her voice became louder. "Now move."

Henry walked in front of Nelda all the way to the study, wondering if he was going to feel the bullet that hit him. When he reached his recliner, he sat. He didn't know what was coming next, but he knew that the longer he stayed alive, the better his chances were. "Nelda, I don't understand this."

She pulled a pill bottle from the pocket of her fashionable jacket. "I want you to take these—all of them. No need to write a note. It's fairly self-evident. You've thought about it and decided there was no use postponing the inevitable. So, you took your own life."

"Why would I do that, Nelda? I've decided to fight this thing. My surgery is scheduled for next—"

"Anyone can change their mind. And if you're wondering about the label on this pill bottle, there isn't one. I doubt the police will bother to check the fingerprints on it, but if they do, they'll find yours. When I close your cold, dead hand around this, everything will end perfectly."

"I'm won't do this, Nelda. I'm not committing suicide."

"Then I'll shoot you. I'll rig it to look like a home invasion in which you ended up being shot. After you're dead, I'll go through the house, take money and jewelry, create a mess, then leave." Nelda didn't flinch as she described what she planned. "Either way, the million-dollar insurance policy you carry on yourself, payable to Claude, will pay off. And he can use the money to replace what he's been stealing from the practice."

"How did you know…"

"I checked. You've had it long enough that it will pay no matter how you die. Suicide or home invasion, it doesn't matter to me."

Nelda held out the bottle. Henry reached forth a trembling hand to take the amber vial. But as he took it, he saw Jean in the doorway of the room. She had taken off her shoes and now tip-toed toward Nelda. If Jean created a distraction, could he spring from the chair and get the pistol away from Claude's wife before she pulled the trigger?

"I think the policeman behind you has heard enough," Henry said.

"You don't expect me to fall for that trick, do you?"

That was when Jean threw the book she had taken from the shelf behind her—not at Nelda, but rather toward the drapes covering the window to Henry's right. Nelda turned slightly, the gun tracked away from him, and he lunged out of his chair toward her, hitting her the way he used to tackle runners when he played cornerback for his college several decades ago.

He had thought he could knock the gun barrel upward, then wrest the pistol away from the woman. He'd figured that between the element of surprise and her sex, he could disarm Nelda. Unfortunately, that was proving no easy task. It took all Henry's might, using both hands, to bend her arm back until the gun barrel was pointed upward. But he couldn't hold it there.

He summoned up strength he didn't know he had. His arm shook with the effort, but Nelda was winning. He watched the barrel of the gun slowly come back down until it was pointing at his face. He squeezed his eyes shut, waiting for the shot.

But the sound never came. Instead, Nelda's head snapped back, and a harsh gurgle came from her. Henry watched as she tried to insert the fingers of her free hand under the cord that was looped around her head to encircle her neck. "Stop ..." she said in a raspy voice.

Instead, Jean, who had both her hands on the cord, must have pulled even harder. As Nelda struggled, Henry managed to move the barrel of the revolver from its position near his face, eventually pointing it toward the ceiling. Finally, he felt her grip on the gun loosen as she seemed to stop struggling for breath. He grabbed the pistol and rolled away, letting Nelda's body fall forward.

"Jean, you can stop now. We don't want to kill her."

"I don't know exactly what was going on, but I could tell what she was going to do." Jean was still breathing hard.

Henry found that his hand trembled as he pointed the pistol toward Nelda. He took a deep breath. "I don't know how you got in, but you're quite literally a lifesaver."

"I found the front door open. There was a woman's loud voice coming from the study, so I decided to be quiet as I approached."

Henry recalled Nelda reaching back with her foot to kick the door shut. She must not have managed to get it fully closed. "Where did you get that cord you used to choke her?"

"This lamp," Jean said. "I hope I didn't crack it, but it was the first thing I could find to use."

"No problem. I think Nelda and Claude gave it to us as a wedding present, and I've always hated it.

Nelda moaned and slowly moved one arm.

"I'll hold the revolver on her," he said. "You call 9-1-1."

Caden had his key out, ready to enter his father's house, but found the door unlocked. He hurried in, with Beth right behind him. "Dad, where are you?"

"In here, in the study."

When Beth and Caden entered the room, they found Henry and Jean waiting for them. Two policemen were also there, but Caden ignored them, rushing to hug his father.

"Dad, we came as soon as we could. Are you okay?"

Beth added her own greeting, then said, "Are you sure you're not hurt?"

"I'm fine." Henry looked at the woman who stood beside him. "I wasn't going to bother you, but Jean insisted."

"I'm glad she did," Caden said. "And I'm glad you listened to her. Sometimes you need a woman telling you the right thing to do." He looked at Beth, who was smiling. "We both do."

One of the two policemen approached Henry. "We're headed out now. The detectives have already gone. Things look secure here. Can you make it down to police headquarters tomorrow about ten to sign a statement?"

"I'll be there. And thanks." Henry waited until the front door closed. "Why don't we sit down so I can answer your questions?"

Caden and Beth started to take the sofa, but Jean and Henry were already heading there, so they sat in chairs across from them.

"Dad, why did Mrs. Horner do this?"

"When Claude and I started the practice, we decided that if either of us died, the other would need money to keep things going," Henry said. "That's why we took out two one million-dollar key-man policies. Apparently, Claude has been dipping into the practice finances, and he feared that if… that when I died, any audit would turn up the shortage. When he found out what I had—and he suspected it long before I told him—Claude was relieved. Statistics being what they are, he knew I'd probably die soon. And he was going to use the money from that policy to repay what he'd taken from the practice."

"You mean *embezzled*, don't you?" Caden said.

"I don't like to use that word, but yes."

"Did Dr. Horner know his wife was going to do this?" Caden asked.

"I doubt it. Nelda sounded like she was acting on her own. But we'll see." Henry grimaced. "I'd imagine the police are bringing Claude in for a not-so-nice interview right now."

"And Mrs. Horner?" Beth asked. "Do you think she'll confess? I'd hate to see you have to go through a trial."

"Nelda will be checked over at the hospital, and then they'll transfer her to a holding cell. I suspect Claude will be ready to tell police what they want, but whether he's ready to implicate his wife, I don't know. Either way, they're both looking at some serious jail time."

"How about your practice?" Caden asked. "Do I need to plan on coming over and dealing with your patients?"

"You've got a hole in your own practice to fill now that Dr. Russell is out of the picture," Henry said. "I can handle my problems, and I suspect you'll be able to take care of yours." He winked. "God has a way of working these things out."

"This is nice," Caden said, and meant it. A month had passed since both he and his dad had narrowly escaped death. They had just marked Henry's recovery from his surgery by attending the services of the First Community Church of Freeman, and now his father and Jean were joining him and Beth for Sunday lunch.

Henry, as expected, had complained because of the trouble he was causing. "We can't eat together. I have some dietary restrictions after my surgery. I'm able to eat solid food now, within reason, but I have to avoid sugar, fats, and fiber."

"We realize that," Jean said. "Beth and I put our heads together, and I can assure you the food we put on the table will be fine for you. We're just happy you're doing so well."

After Henry said grace that managed to cover the food, his recovery so far, and several other things, the four began to pass dishes around.

Caden looked at his dad and felt a thrill of prayers answered, lives changed, and safety despite attempts to kill half the people seated around the table. "Dad, I just can't believe Nelda Horner would do such a thing. Or, for that matter, Claude Horner."

Henry looked distrustfully at what appeared to be mashed potatoes. But Jean and Beth had assured him everything on the table was compatible with his diet, so he helped himself to some. "I wish Claude had told me he needed money, instead of stealing it from the practice."

Beth accepted the bowl from Henry, helped herself, and passed it to Jean.

Jean paused, holding the food. "Will he be charged as an accessory to attempted murder, or what?"

"Both Nelda and Claude Horner invoked their right to remain silent and insisted on legal representation. Since they're married, they can't be compelled to testify against each other. Right now, their attorneys are looking for a deal. Meanwhile, accountants are going over our books," Henry said. "I'm sure they'll both be serving long sentences when it's all over." He tasted the material he'd just put on his plate and discovered that what he was eating was mashed cauliflower. "Not bad."

"What did you do about your practice?" Caden asked.

Henry swallowed another mouthful and followed it with a sip of iced tea. He'd learned to drink it without sugar, and although it was no substitute for the sweet tea he preferred, he'd adjust. "For the immediate future, some of my colleagues have offered to do the procedures already scheduled by Claude and me if the patients are willing. They'll also take care of post-op appointments."

"What about long term?" Caden asked.

"Got it covered," Henry said. "Yesterday I talked to a young surgeon who's interested in the practice." He paused to take another sip of tea. "In our initial conversation, I said Claude and I needed him to come in with us because of my illness. Today I asked him how he'd like to take over the whole thing."

"And his answer?"

"Once he decided I wasn't kidding, he told me he was very interested. He'll call me back tomorrow, but it looks good."

Jean looked around the table and seemed to relax when she saw everyone enjoying the food. "Caden, what have you done after Dr. Russell ... er ... left the practice suddenly?"

Caden blotted his lips with his napkin. "You mean since her arrest? Dr. Sparling and I divided up her patients, which was a bit of a stretch initially, but we've got it covered. A woman who graduated from the surgery residency program where I trained is coming up next weekend to look over the practice."

Beth chimed in. "And she's happily married to an anesthesiologist. I think there's room for both of them to take over Ann's space."

"What about you, Dad? Dr. Ross has kept me in the loop after your surgery, but we haven't gotten into specifics."

Henry put down his silverware, used his napkin, and looked around the table. "Dr. Markham thinks the Whipple procedure was successful. Dr. Ross talked to me about adding post-op chemotherapy or radiation. Studies vary on whether it would be helpful. I told him anything that gave me a better chance of making that five-year survival group would be worthwhile, even if there are side effects."

Beth suddenly excused herself and left the table. Despite attempts by the others to keep the conversation going, they all heard the faint retching noises that issued from the bathroom. Eventually, they heard a toilet flush, water run, and a door open and close.

"Sorry," Beth said as she took her seat.

Caden frowned. "Hon, you had to leave church a couple of times this morning, and that's the second time since we got here that you've had to run to the bathroom. Are you okay?"

Beth looked around the table and smiled. "I'm okay, but I think I'll need to see a doctor in the next week or two."

"Can it wait that long?" Henry asked.

"As I understand it, what I have is pretty normal and generally self-limited." She turned her attention to Caden. "But I think it's time you started interviewing for a nurse to take my place."

"Why? Don't you like working with me? Was it something I did?"

Beth snickered. "Sort of." Then she looked at Henry. "I'm glad things are going well with you. Because I want to see the expression on your face when you first hold your new grandchild."

WATCH FOR MY NEXT NOVELLA, EMERGENCY CASE, RELEASING THIS WINTER

D r. Kelly Irving strode from her house into the attached garage. She headed for her car, still fuming. Here it was, December 13, less than two weeks before Christmas, but she wasn't in a holiday mood—not even after the snow that fell last night.

The garage was cold, and she knew her car would be as well, so Kelly shrugged deeper into her coat. Of course, it was December, so what else should she expect? Here in this part of Texas, snow on the ground for Christmas was unusual, but it had come overnight—at least a smattering of the white stuff. Would it be a white Christmas? Frankly, she didn't care.

Kelly climbed into her car. She gave a glance to her husband's BMW sitting to her right. Jack should be coming out of the house any minute, but right now Kelly didn't care about him. Not after the fight they'd had.

She pushed the button to open the garage door, then started her Subaru sedan. Kelly looked in the rearview mirror and briefly reflected that the snow on the roof of the house directly across the alley from her made the area look Christmas-like. She just wished her attitude were in tune with the season. There might be peace on earth, but not at her house.

Kelly was on automatic pilot as she slipped her car into reverse and backed down the slightly inclined drive. The tires took hold easily, despite the dusting of snow that had fallen during the night, but nevertheless she went slowly, occasionally glancing at the rearview mirror but not bothering to look at the images the car's back-up camera displayed. Suddenly she felt a bump, and the backward motion of her car hesitated, then stopped. Kelly shook her head. *Please, not this morning. I'm already running late.*

She tapped the accelerator, but the obstruction held her car fast. Kelly put the transmission into park and climbed out.

As she made her way carefully to the rear of the car, Kelly hoped the bump she felt was just a mound of snow. A few moments with the shovel could take care of that. She might even be able to simply go forward a bit, then put the car in reverse, push down on the accelerator, power over the obstruction, and be on her way.

But after she'd taken a few more steps toward the car's rear bumper she realized that the bump she'd felt wasn't snow. It was the body of a man lying in the driveway, blocking her passage. His left hand, which lay outstretched beneath the right rear wheel of her still-running car, seemed to be reaching out to her.

She stifled the scream that caught in her throat. Her eyes never left the corpse as she tried to call out. When Kelly finally was able to make her vocal cords work, she called in a surprisingly calm voice, "Jack, there's a dead man in our driveway."

Jack's mind was elsewhere as he walked out of the house and into the garage. When he felt the cold wind and saw that the overhead door was open, he grumbled and buttoned his topcoat. The sight of Kelly's car idling about halfway down the driveway caused him to shake his head sadly. *What has she done this time? And is it going to slow me down?*

"What's wrong?" Jack said in a voice calculated to carry. "If it's car trouble, you'll have to call AAA. And don't think you're going to take mine. I'm due in court for a very important hearing this morning." He started to open the door and climb into his BMW but stopped when he heard Kelly's words. At first, he wasn't certain he'd heard her correctly.

"Jack, there's a dead man in our driveway."

"What?"

She repeated the sentence, a bit louder this time. Jack left his car and moved toward the back of Kelly's Subaru. "That's ridiculous," he said.

"See for yourself," she managed to say.

In a few more steps, he reached the corpse. When he saw the face, he knew this was going to be a long morning—no, make that a long day.

Books by Richard L. Mabry, MD

Novels of Medical Suspense
Code Blue
Medical Error
Diagnosis Death
Lethal Remedy
Stress Test
Heart Failure
Critical Condition
Fatal Trauma
Miracle Drug
Medical Judgment
Cardiac Event
Guarded Prognosis

Novellas
Rx Murder
Silent Night, Deadly Night
Doctor's Dilemma
Surgeon's Choice

Non-Fiction
The Tender Scar: Life After the Death of A Spouse

WHAT OTHERS HAVE SAID ABOUT RICHARD MABRY'S BOOKS

About *Cardiac Event:* "There is so much action in his latest release, with just the right amount of romance, it makes it hard to go on without finishing one more chapter."
Romantic Times Book Reviews (4 ½ stars, Top Pick)

About *Medical Judgment*: "Balances action with emotion and struggles of faith, making it easy for readers to care about the characters and what happens to them in all the twists and turns of the genre."
Lauraine Snelling, best-selling author of the Red River of the North sagas

About *Miracle Drug*: "Excellent story. Excellently crafted. Great characters. Great plot." DiAnne Mills, Christy-award winning author of *Deadlock*

About *Fatal Trauma*: "Asks big questions of faith, priorities, and meaning, all within the context of a tightly crafted medical drama."
Steven James, best-selling author of *Placebo* and *Checkmate*

About *Critical Condition*: "Has the uncommon ability to take medical details and make them understandable, while still maintaining accuracy and intrigue."
Romantic Times Book Reviews (4 ½ stars)

About *Heart Failure*: "Combines his medical expertise with a story that will keep you on the edge of your seat."
USA Today

About *Stress Test*: "Original and profound. I found the … story (moving) a mile a minute."
Michael Palmer, *NYT* best-selling author of *Oath of Office*

Made in the USA
Monee, IL
06 November 2019